ALSO BY NANCY GOTTER GATES

A Stroke of Misfortune

Happy reading!

When **PUSH** Comes to Death

Nancy Gotter Gates

Nancy Gotter Gates

Book design by Karen Gates

Published by Alabaster Book Publishing, Kernersville, NC

www.publisheralabaster.biz

Library of Congress Catalgoing in Publication Data

2007924200

Printed in the United States of America

ISBN 978-0-9790949-7-2

For my sister, Carolyn

ACKNOWLEDGMENTS

I'm always indebted to past and present members of my writers' group for their invaluable advice. This includes Diane Berry, Betty DiMeo, Helen Goodman, Wendy Greene, Dorothy O'Neill and Carla Buckley.

And a special thanks to my daughter,
Karen Gates, for the design of this book.

Chapter *one*

Some days at Stewardship Life go slower than others, and this was definitely one of them. I'd managed to complete two of the easier *New York Times* crossword puzzles since anyone had called. Logan, my boss and the only other person who worked here, was out charming potential customers. And I was caught up on my filing and data entry and bored out of my mind. Finally in the middle of the afternoon, the phone rang breaking the cursed silence.

"I'm calling to report a death," the familiar voice said. It was my ex-husband. I'd know that tone of self importance anywhere, any time. Even though we hadn't seen each other in some months, I'd been married to the sorry bastard for thirty-three years. Then he decided that one of the associates at the law firm of Carruther, Mierjeski and Poag would feed his ego better than I could at my advanced age of fifty-five years. She, of course, was young enough to be our daughter—if we had one—which we didn't since I'd been unable to have kids. Maybe that's what it was all about, but I doubted it. Bernard was too self absorbed to regret that he wasn't a father.

"Bernard, for heaven's sake! It's me, Tommi."

After a second's hesitation he said, "Oh, that's right. I knew you worked for some insurance agency, but I can never remember which one." No "Hi there, how are you?"

If that wasn't typical. If it wasn't related to him or his law firm, it wasn't worth remembering. Out of sight, out of mind, and I'd been out of his sight for over a year.

"Well, how are you anyway?" I said, simply for the sake of politeness. I'd decided from the get-go that I'd try very hard to be gracious whenever I had contact with him, which I prayed would be as seldom as possible. Being ugly to him would only confirm in his mind that he had done the right thing. But then Bernard never had doubts about any of his actions.

"Fine, fine," he said, impatient with the niceties.

"Me too," I said, though he hadn't asked, pretending that he cared.

"Good. Now about the death claim..."

"Okay," I sighed, glad I no longer had to fake cheerfulness. "What's the name of the deceased?"

"Oscar T. Sellars."

I was struck dumb. Finally I found my voice again. "Oh my God! Do you mean Cap Sellars? Nina's husband?" I couldn't believe this.

"How do you know them?" His tone was accusatory, as if I had no right to their acquaintance.

"But he wasn't that old!" I said. I was sure Cap was considerably younger than I was. "Did he have a heart attack or a car accident?"

"No," he said gruffly. "Nothing like that. I didn't realize you were friends," he persisted. He just wasn't going to let it go. His proprietary manner really pissed me off.

"Nina came into the office to transfer their files from California three months ago," I said. "We made the connection when she saw my name was Poag, and we've been getting together regularly. In fact, I was supposed to meet Cap this weekend. You knew he'd just gotten back from Hollywood, didn't you? Oh, Bernard, this is terrible! What happened?"

Bernard couldn't let go of resenting the fact that I knew them. "She never mentioned to me that she'd met you." I could see him pouting in my mind's eye. When he divorced me, did that mean that the whole family including cousins was off limits?

"She had the good sense not to discuss you with me or bring up my name in front of you once we figured out our relationship. But for God's sake, *tell me!!*" How could I have forgotten how utterly exasperating he could be? But there was no sense in dwelling on all his annoying quirks. Particularly since I didn't have to endure them any more.

"They had just pulled onto a boat ramp on Lake Brandt last night when a car or truck came up from behind and pushed their car into the water. She managed to get out and dog paddle to shore. Unfortunately Cap was too inebriated and couldn't get his seatbelt undone. The rescue squad was able to resuscitate him, but he died a little later in the hospital."

"Oh, no. Poor Nina!" The horror of it was inconceivable. I kept trying to picture it in my mind, the panic Nina must have felt. My own deep fear of water made Nina's terrifying experience tangible to me.

"Tommi, are you still there?"

I tried to calm myself by taking a deep breath. "Okay, Bernard. Let's see. Logan's out right now, and I'm not sure how a case like this will be handled. I'll have him give you a call just as soon as possible."

"Please do that."

"I must call Nina. Do you know if she's home?"

"I think she's making funeral arrangements. You can probably reach her to-night."

I tried repeatedly to call Nina the rest of the afternoon, but all I got was Cap's voice, eerily responding on the answering machine. I left a message to call me at work before five or at home after that, but the call never came.

I rushed home after work to catch the 5:30 local news. At the door, Tee-nine-cy, my twenty-pound Maine Coon cat, Tee for short, greeted me with his usual feline detachment, then made a beeline to his food bowl waving his coon-striped tail happily as I measured the cat food. I pulled a frozen dinner out of the fridge and tossed it into the microwave, turning on the TV as it heated.

Cap's death was the lead story. As Nina's picture flashed on the screen, Liz Covington, WFMY-TV co-anchor began, "Police arrested Nina Sellars of Oak Ridge about thirty minutes ago and charged her with murder in connection with the death of her husband, Oscar T. Sellars, well-known screenwriter who penned a number of movies, including two Oscar nominees." A videotape showing a black Jaguar being towed out of the water under floodlights accompanied her story. Nina drove a tan BMW, so it must have been Cap's car.

"Mrs. Sellars claims that someone unknown pushed their car into Lake Brandt last night around midnight as she and her husband sat inside it on a boat ramp," Liz continued. "According to police, Mrs. Sellars said she was driving because Mr. Sellars was intoxicated, and she was unable to prevent the car from going into the water. But police say they have evidence Mrs. Sellars is directly responsible for the death. They are not releasing any details at this time."

This was totally unbelievable. Nina wasn't capable of such an act. She was too crazy about Cap, in spite of his infidelities, to even think of harming him. She'd put up with his straying eye for a long time, but she'd told me that things were turning in her favor, and she was sure her marriage was getting back on track. Besides, she was a loving and caring soul to whom violence was an anathema.

I decided to call Bernard; something I hadn't done since our divorce was finalized, hoping he could fill me in on what was going on. But there was no answer either at his home or his office. I was sure he was working after hours as he had always done, but the phones weren't answered after five p.m.

Chapter *two*

It had been early June when Nina Sellars first came to my office. It had been another one of those slow days, and I was delighted for a break in the tedium. Logan Stahl, my boss, was at a regional meeting for Stewardship Life agents.

Nina, not much over five feet tall, had the slender build of a teenager, but I pegged her to be in her mid-thirties. Her oval face was dominated by large green eyes with a downward slope that gave a tinge of sadness to her expression, and her hair was as blonde as a tow-headed child. It didn't seem possible it was her natural color, but the bleach job was masterfully done. She was dressed in an expensive-looking sweater with appliqués of pale yellow flowers and matching silk skirt with a flounce at the bottom, definitely not the tailored look affected by the well-dressed of Greensboro.

"My husband and I moved to North Carolina from California last year," she said. "Never thought about getting a local agent until I got this bill for our annual premium." She held out an envelope to me. "Cap's been talking about increasing his insurance, so I figured I'd better find out how to get our files transferred from L.A."

I took out the statement. It was made out to Oscar T. Sellars and was for the premium on a million-dollar Whole Life policy. I was impressed, to put it mildly. Logan had on occasion sold term life policies for this amount, but I'd never seen a Whole Life one this large. Since they build up cash reserves, they cost considerably more.

I pulled a form out of the top file drawer. "If you'll have him sign a policy-owner authorization form, we'll have all your records transferred here."

"That's it?"

"That's it. Nothing to it. Mr. Stahl will give you a call when the transfer's complete."

Suddenly she pointed to the placard on the front of my desk. "Tommi Poag? Could you by any chance be related to Bernard Poag?"

I almost flinched. "Not any more, thank God, though I used to be married to him," I said without thinking, then realized I should watch my mouth. Not a good idea to be so blunt when I didn't know how she knew him or if they were friends.

But it didn't seem to faze her. "What a small world," she said. "I'm Frank Poag's daughter, Nina Sellars. Dad is Bernard's first cousin."

"Frank Poag, huh?" It took me a few seconds to place him. Then I remembered: he was the cousin Bernard refused to acknowledge. "I'm afraid I never met him," I said, wondering whether to bring up the estrangement or not. I only learned of this cousin when a distant relative of Bernard's asked about him once.

"He doesn't exist as far as I am concerned," Bernard had replied sharply. I never could get another word out of him about Frank.

"I'm not surprised you don't know him, since as far as I know they haven't spoken in over thirty years. Isn't that ridiculous?" Nina shrugged and sighed. "Guys. I don't understand them."

As much as I didn't feel like discussing Bernard, I'd always been curious about that estrangement and wondered what could have caused such bitterness. Waving towards the chair beside my desk I asked, "Have you got a minute? I'd really love to get to the bottom of that feud. And besides, it would be nice to get acquainted with you. Since Bernard is no longer in my life, he can't object."

"Sure." Nina dropped her purse on the floor and sat down. "This feels good," she said clasping her hands behind her head and stretching. "I've been shopping all day and I'm bushed."

"So tell me about those two. I didn't even know Frank existed until several years ago, and Bernard refused to tell me why he had such a grudge."

Nina shook her head. "Wish I could enlighten you, but Dad would never talk about it either. The funny thing is, Dad lives in Wisconsin now, and I've gotten to know Bernard quite well since we moved back from California. We consulted him on some legal matters when we bought our house, and he's bent over backward helping us get settled in."

"Oh, really?" I said. Obviously I did need to watch my mouth. But that surprised me because it was so unlike Bernard. Altruism had never been his thing. Maybe he was courting them so they'd choose him as their lawyer in all matters. With her husband's obvious wealth, that would be a big incentive.

Nina seemed to sense my skepticism. She smiled sympathetically and said, "Well, I'm sure you don't feel the least bit kindly toward him, but I will tell you this: he's told me a couple of times how bad he felt about hurting you."

I let out an uncontrollable snort, a mixture of disbelief and contempt. "Oh, sure. Yeah." What a crock, I thought.

"Look, I know how you feel. I've been through the fire myself. Just one more thing about Bernard, and then we'll change the subject. I still don't know what's going on with him and Dad. I brought it up just once, and he quickly changed the subject. So there you are. The Poag family mystery."

"As you said: men. Who can figure them out?" I shook my head and wondered what she meant by "having been through the fire herself."

Nina glanced at her watch. "Oh, sorry, I've kept you past closing time. Look, it'd really be fun to get to know you better. After all, you were part of the family for years, and if it hadn't been for those childish guys, we'd have probably been good friends long ago. My husband's out in California for a while. He's a screenwriter, and right now he's up to his eyeballs rewriting a script that's in production. Do you have any plans for dinner?"

"The usual. Pop a frozen one in the microwave."

"How about being my guest at the Green Valley Grill?"

For a brief second, I hesitated. Did I really want to get chummy with someone who was close to Bernard? But then I acknowledged that Nina had nothing to do with our rotten relationship. Why take it out on her? She seemed very nice. And I sure as heck didn't get dinner invitations every day.

"My stomach may not know how to react to a non-frozen meal," I said smiling. "But I'm willing to take the challenge. Just let me fill out this form so your husband can sign it, and I'll be ready to go." I hadn't been anywhere near a restaurant as nice as the Green Valley Grill in over a year. My budget permitted little more than fast food dining.

It was an overcast and humid June day in Greensboro. I was surprised at how muggy it had become since that morning. I'd brought a sandwich from home for lunch so I hadn't been outside since 8:30. Nina offered to drive in her BMW, so we left my car, a ten-year-old Mitsubishi wagon, in the parking lot to be picked up later.

When we were seated in the restaurant, Nina leaned across the table and said, "I'm jealous of your red hair. I get so tired of having my roots touched up."

I smiled and said, "Thanks," determined not to reveal that I was born a blah brunette. I'd spent my life apologizing for my supposed shortcomings and denigrating my assets, just as so many other ego-challenged women have done. When I divorced, I made up my mind never again to disparage myself in any way. I would accept all compliments in good grace and would never admit to any help from beauticians, padded undergarments, creams, lotions or any more drastic means I might have to resort to. And if I decided to let it all go and not fight it, I wouldn't apologize for that either.

When our meals had been served, we began the exchange of information that defined our lives as women have done since time immemorial.

"Do you have any children, Tommi?" she asked.

" 'Fraid not," I said. I didn't elaborate because I didn't want to talk about one of the saddest chapters of my life.

"Neither do I. I had a couple of miscarriages and finally a hysterectomy. In hindsight, it was probably one of those unnecessary ones."

"I'm so sorry," I said. Already I felt a strong kinship with this woman in spite of our age difference. There's a sort of informal but powerful connection amongst women who badly want children yet are unable to have them, a relationship forged by a mutual sense of loss. Only someone in our shoes can truly understand our pain.

But Nina didn't want to dwell on that any more than I did.

"How long have you worked for Stewardship Life, Tommi?" she asked.

"About a year. Since shortly after the divorce." I was savoring the prosciutto wrapped scallops, wishing I had a job that would permit me to eat like this regularly.

"A way to keep busy and keep your mind off things, I guess."

"A way to keep food on the table. I used most of my settlement to buy a condominium. Bought it outright because I wasn't too sure about my ability to support myself, and I didn't want big mortgage payments. Good thing I did. My job isn't exactly top drawer on the pay scale. My main concern is if I'll ever be able to retire." Actually, that was a recurring nightmare with me. Would I still be working when I was eighty-five?

"How did you end up in the insurance field?" Nina might be tiny, but she was way ahead of me in cleaning her plate of lamb chops and couscous. I didn't see how she could still eat so daintily while the food disappeared like a time-lapse photo.

I wanted to say because of my extraordinary talents, but decided to tell the truth instead. "Because I groveled a lot. I practically threw myself on Logan's mercy. Truth is, Nina, the only time I'd worked was as a secretary when I was putting Bernard through law school. During our marriage I did volunteer work which didn't cut much ice with the human resources types. I got a Liberal Arts degree years ago and had a year of law school which is pretty useless now."

"I didn't know that!" Nina put down her fork in surprise.

"Oh, yes. I quit to marry Bernard and put *him* through law school."

Nina shook her head and reached over to pat my hand. "That sucks."

"Amen," I said. "Now you know about me, what about you? How'd you end up in California?"

"I went to UCLA. Met Cap my senior year and was gaga over him, dropped out, and got married. That was sixteen years ago. He'd been in the screen-writing program and was desperately trying to break into Hollywood."

"I've heard it's really tough. Doesn't half the country think they can write for the movies?"

"Yeah. We had pretty rough going for a number of years. I waitressed to help out, but he finally got his foot in the door when they bought a script he'd called *The Raid*. They changed it to *The Downfall of John McCormick*. Stupid title."

"Sorry. I don't remember that."

"Neither does anyone else. The direction was terrible, and the cast was a bunch of unknowns. But it was a start. He's been quite successful the past seven or eight years even though he's still not that well known generally. It's funny how everyone is familiar with the stars and the directors, but screen writers are usually pretty obscure. But you couldn't have a movie without them. And the quality of the screenplay makes or breaks the movie."

"Well, then, why did you move back here? Doesn't he need to be in Hollywood?"

Nina blushed slightly and played with her fork, twirling it upright on her now empty plate.. "It's on account of me. Well, at least I *thought* it was for me. Now I'm not so sure." She did not elaborate, but continued playing with her fork and staring at her plate.

I didn't want to push it. Nina was obviously in some kind of distress, so I picked up the menu to check the desserts. "Wow. Look, they have Frozen Nutty Irishman. Are you game? How about splitting a piece?"

Nina smiled again. "Sure, why not?"

The subject of moving from California seemed to have been dropped. The waiter brought a huge piece of diet-busting chocolate cake with Irish cream mousse and crushed English toffee which we divided it in half. We both ate in silence, savoring the moist, delectable richness of each bite. The cure for unhappiness is always chocolate.

"Well now," I said as I wiped my mouth after scraping every last morsel from the plate, "I should be going to aerobics class tonight instead of yoga after this. Sitting in the lotus position isn't going to take off all these calories." I looked at my watch. "It's 6:30 now and the class starts at 7:30, and I have to go home and change first."

"I've always wanted to learn yoga," Nina said as she searched in her billfold for her charge card. "Any chance I could go with you sometime?"

"Why not tonight?"

"I live on the north side of Oak Ridge. That's too far to go to get changed and get back in time." Oak Ridge is a small town north of Greensboro.

"I'll loan you some sweats. Luckily they have a string-tie waist since you're a couple of sizes smaller than I am." More like three sizes maybe?

Nina was all smiles now. "I'd love that."

I sensed that she badly wanted to establish a friendship. And I welcomed the idea of having a new friend in my life. Many of my married chums drifted away after my divorce—as if I were a threat to their marriages. Although I knew that was not uncommon, it hurt all the same. I felt like wearing a sign on my chest: *not interested in used goods.*

As we left the restaurant for my condo, I wondered if Nina would ever confide in me why the move from California was so painful.

Chapter
three

On Friday Nina called to invite me to her house in Oak Ridge.

"I don't know about you," she said, "but the weekends are the hardest to get through when I'm alone. I thought maybe you'd like to come out tomorrow for lunch and a swim in the pool. Or maybe I should say a chance to get your feet wet since it's only four feet deep."

"I'd love that." I felt as if I had a reprieve. The next day was the first anniversary of my divorce, and I'd been tempted to stay in bed all day with the covers over my head. But I knew I'd be much better off with company. We could talk about the economy, the state of the world, or gossip about movie stars–anything to distract me.

I was totally unprepared for Nina's house. I'd supposed it would be very nice, but I hadn't expected a mansion. It was on the outskirts of Oak Ridge, a town of four thousand or so, and sat high upon the crest of a perfectly rounded hill surrounded by more than a dozen majestic oak trees. Since I seldom strayed off the two main streets of the town, Highways 68 and 150, I had never passed it. There was no other structure in Oak Ridge remotely as splendid, although there were many fine homes. The interior of her home was even more beautiful than the outside. The spacious rooms were filled with exquisite Williamsburg-era antiques in a palette of pastels.

As lovely as it was, I could not imagine living there. It would seem too much like walking into the pages of *Architectural Digest*. I envisioned Tee sharpening his claws on the pale pink sofa. He would have a heyday demolishing the fabrics there.

I followed Nina as she headed back through the kitchen to the family room, the only place, at least downstairs, where one could comfortably relax and put up her feet. It was two stories high with a window wall framing a magnificent view over rolling fields and woodlands. This room was furnished with oversized down-filled chairs and matching sofas with accessories that obviously had been picked up from travels around the world: Maori wood carvings, African baskets, all sorts of colorful and intriguing objects.

Nina led me through one of the French doors that made up the lower tier of windows out onto an expansive deck that surrounded a large irregular-shaped pool. She had lunch already set up on a glass and wrought-iron table in the shade of a tulip poplar. The deck had been constructed around the tree trunk.

"This is gorgeous," I said. "I had no idea there was such a place here. Did you guys build it?"

"No," Nina laughed, "Some guy who made a fortune in tech stocks. For years he refused to move out of his old house in the middle of town. Finally his wife nagged him into building this when their daughter was getting married. They tore down an old farmhouse on this spot so they could have all these beautiful trees. That was four or five years ago. Well, shortly after the wedding, the wife got cancer and died. They say he lost the will to live after that and only lasted another year."

"How sad. The daughter didn't want it?"

"Her husband is a politician in Colorado. No way they can live in North Carolina."

"So they put it on the market. This isn't a town you would think of to look for a house like this." Oak Ridge was originally known for its military academy. The older homes were mostly modest but in recent years, fine new housing developments were popping up. But none of them compared to Nina's.

"You're right. That's why the place had been on the market for a long time when we saw it. Cap had been looking for a house in Greensboro for months but couldn't find anything he liked. And we got a bundle for our house in California, so of course Cap wanted to splurge it all on a new one. There wasn't much in our price range."

I had no doubt about that. The price of a house in Greensboro was probably no more than a third of what a similar house would sell for in California.

"Anyway, Cap isn't above flaunting it. I personally would have liked something a lot smaller. I mean this is kind of ridiculous for two people to have all this space, and it's hard to find help out here. But living like this gets the attention of the 'in' crowd in Greensboro. I hate to say it, but Cap eats it up when they make over him because he knows movie stars and producers and directors. He loves partying and hanging out with those people."

"You sound as if you're not crazy about it."

"No, for one thing, he always drinks too much. For another, I'm not too comfortable with those women. I didn't grow up wearing designer clothes and going to private school. Sometimes I think they're only nice to me because I'm Cap's wife."

"That's silly, Nina. Why wouldn't they like you for yourself? I was impressed by you the minute I met you." It was bad enough that my sense of self worth had been pummeled so this past year. This lovely young woman didn't need to be so insecure. On the surface, it seemed she had everything going for her.

"You're sweet, Tommi. And good for the ego. I guess I've always felt I existed in Cap's shadow. Especially now that he's successful."

I wanted to shake her and tell her she was probably worth three Caps. Instead I said, "Well, you need to get over that. I fell into that trap, too, and you know where that puts you when you no longer have a husband. In total identity crisis."

Nina had prepared a delicious lunch of crab salad, homemade rolls, and a wonderful blackberry cobbler.

When I exclaimed over the meal, she offered to share her recipes.

"Thanks, but no thanks, " I said. "I really loathe to cook, especially for one. I really meant it when I said I live on frozen dinners."

"What did you do about cooking when you were married?"

I felt my throat tighten and tears well up, and before I realized it, they began to course down my cheeks. I picked up my napkin to wipe them away, completely astounded at myself. I hadn't expected to do that and felt like a fool.

"I'm sorry," Nina said anxiously, touching my arm. "What did I say?"

I began to laugh through my tears. "Nothing at all. I am such a wimp. It's the first anniversary of my divorce today, and it's gotten to me. I guess I should celebrate that I'm rid of him, but it still hurts. I just had to wallow in self pity for a minute there."

"You're allowed. Especially the way it happened."

"It's pretty hard on the ego when he falls in love with someone young enough to be your daughter."

"Yes, I've met Pamela of course."

Oh, Lord, that was right. If Nina had become close to Bernard, she probably would be close to Pamela too. I wished I hadn't run my mouth. This was very awkward.

"Pamela is okay, I suppose," Nina went on, "but she can't hold a candle to you, Tommi."

Did she really mean that or was she simply trying to make me feel better?

She went on. "I think the attraction was that they're both with the same firm, and Bernard is so wrapped up in his work that she's just sort of an extension of it. They can discuss it all night long." She started to giggle. "Can't you just see it? In the middle of a passionate embrace he says to her 'Darling, did you get the deposition on the Jones case?' Their idea of rapture is probably quizzing each other on arcane judicial rulings."

"I'd heard that she wanted to be made a partner more than anything else," I said, "and she thought snagging Bernard would be her ticket." One of the other partner's wives had actually told me that.

"That's possible," Nina said. "Some women will go to any length to get what they want whether it's money, position or whatever." She looked out across the fields, her eyes far away, her demeanor sad. She sat silent for a couple of minutes, then said, "I'm more or less in the same boat. Cap's been having an affair."

"Oh, Nina." So this was the source of her insecurity.

"I only learned about her a few months ago, but I think it's gone on for a year and a half or longer. You know when you asked me the other day why we moved from California?"

"Yes?"

"I never liked it out there. I'd always been homesick for the East. But I knew that in order to get his career established, Cap needed to be where the action was. But now that he's doing so well, it doesn't really matter where he lives. People come to him. Besides, there's a lot of film making going on in North Carolina now."

"True." We were right behind California and New York in the production of films.

"I'd been after him to move back here. He ignored me for the longest time, and then suddenly he decided to do it. I was so thrilled. I thought it was for my sake."

"It wasn't?"

"A few months ago I found out that he'd been having an affair with someone named Allison. When I confronted him, he admitted to it. But he wouldn't tell me any more than that. No last name. Nothing about where she lived. But it seemed pretty obvious that he was seriously thinking about dumping me. I think he moved me here so that I'd at least be back home when he left me."

Oh, God, I thought, another two-timing husband. Were any of them faithful? "Why do you think he won't tell you her full name?"

"Two possible reasons. One, that I might contact her and raise hell. Two, that she might be someone famous, maybe an actress, and he doesn't want it to leak out. I've figured out she's in New York from little things he's said."

"Well, I guess you're glad she's not in L.A. since he's there now."

"You bet. Normally he goes to New York fairly often on business, but right now he's stuck in California. Hopefully that's keeping him away from her. Anyway, ever since I found out, I've been doing everything I can to improve our relationship, and I honestly think things are beginning to turn around. Of course, he might be trying to keep me off balance, but he seems more loving lately. Anyway, our sex life sure has improved." She blushed and laughed. "I guess that's the usual measure for these things, isn't it?"

"It was in my case, only it was the other way around. Stupid me. I thought Bernard was having trouble with impotence. Truth was, he was horny as a teenager. Just not with me."

Nina put her hand on top of mine. "I'm really sorry about that."

I just shrugged. No sense dumping on her. Why spoil a beautiful day.

Nina and I saw each other a couple of times a week for the next three months. She was at loose ends with Cap away, and I was always glad for company. She became a regular at my yoga class, and sometimes we would go to a movie or concert together. Often we would just spend an evening at my place playing Scrabble or Rummicube.

At first I felt a little embarrassed to have Nina in my home, it was in such sharp contrast to her mansion. I live in a compact two-story condo with kitchen open to the living area, all one thousand square feet of space, and a fenced-in patio in the back. But Nina seemed very comfortable there. I sometimes felt she liked being there more than she liked staying in her own place. I think all that space must have been intimidating. Particularly when she was alone.

Even Tee warmed up to her immediately, which was something of a miracle because he usually cowers under the bed when I have company. Nina claimed she would love to have a whole menagerie of cats, but Cap was allergic to them.

It became a warm and relaxed friendship between us, and I had mixed feelings about Cap's return which was scheduled for the second week in September. I wondered how often I would see Nina once her husband was home. Since my social life had dwindled to almost nothing since my divorce, I would miss our get-togethers.

Chapter *four*

And then that unbelievable call came about Cap's death. I brooded about Nina's arrest all evening and tried several times without success to reach Bernard. I finally gave up and went to bed but was unable to fall asleep.

After several fruitless hours of tossing and turning, I decided to call Bernard once more, regardless of the time. I had to know what was going on and I didn't care if I ruined his beauty rest.

"It's Tommi," I said, when he finally answered in a groggy voice. "I can't believe what I heard on television. Can you tell me anything about Nina?"

There was a pause, and finally he spoke. "Damn it. Do you realize it's two-thirty?"

"Of course. I couldn't get you earlier, and I had to know about her." I was sitting in my bed, cross-legged, with Tee in my lap. When I couldn't sleep, he couldn't either.

Bernard sounded a little more awake now. "I can't tell you much. But it's not looking good for her."

"My God, Bernard. You know as well as I do that she couldn't have done anything like that. Is she getting a good lawyer?"

He hesitated a couple of seconds. "Actually, she's asked me to represent her."

"What! You've got to be kidding!" I shouted into the phone, causing Tee to jump off my bed in fright. "Bernard, you handle things like wills and trusts and incorporations. You're not a criminal lawyer."

"You're forgetting that I worked in the Public Defender's office for four years. If that isn't valid experience, I don't know what the hell is." He was really awake now and truly pissed.

"Oh, sure," I said, "How could I ever forget that? You kept griping about the lowlifes who rip off society and then expect the taxpayers to underwrite their defense. Such noble-mindedness," I added sarcastically. We had many an argument about that at the time. I was still in my youthful idealistic stage then. Bernard never had one.

"You don't have to be a left-wing do-gooder to be a great lawyer, you know. Remember the Billy Joe Arnold case when everybody thought he'd go to the electric chair, and I got him off scot-free?"

"You never believed he was innocent; you only cared about winning."

"Hell, yes, that's what it's always about, don't kid yourself. I did my job, which was to defend him, and I did it better than most people could. If you'll recall, the department tried like the devil to keep me, but it didn't pay diddly squat. I accomplished what I intended–to make a name for myself so the better law firms would notice me."

"And you didn't want to be a criminal lawyer because socially speaking it's not so acceptable, I know. So what about Nina? Are you taking her case because she can pay big bucks?"

"That's unfair, Tommi. I care about Nina. And I may not make a cent. Everything is in Cap's name. Unless she's cleared, there won't be any money to pay a lawyer. So it's me or the Public Defender's office."

I was amazed. Bernard was really serious about this,. I couldn't remember when he'd had any kind of an emotional investment in a case. Nina had managed to find a soft spot in that normally dispassionate heart of his.

"Look, I want to help in some way," I pleaded. "There has to be something I can do."

"I don't know what that would be." His tone was cold. He wasn't going to give me an inch.

"I had a year of law school, and remember I worked with the crisis line. I was really good with that. People would open up to me."

"What are you getting at?"

"Why don't you let me do some checking with friends and relatives to see what was going on with Cap. Maybe someone wanted him dead. The police seem to have made up their minds Nina is guilty, so I doubt they are looking much further."

"You're not a licensed investigator, Tommi."

"That's true. But I'm sure I could do it. God knows I'm motivated enough. Someone you hired out of the blue wouldn't care about Nina the way I do."

"Sorry, that's just not good enough. I don't think you realize how serious this is. We're not playing games here."

Damn it. Did he have to talk down to me that way? "I'm well aware of that. I've never been more serious in my life."

"Can't do it, Tommi. I know you mean well." He was trying to sound sympathetic, even if he couldn't pull it off. "I'll do everything in my power to get her out of this. You'll have to trust me."

Trust him? He had to be kidding. But I guess I didn't have a choice. "Okay. Sorry to have bothered you, Bernard."

I lay awake for hours after that, regretting that I'd called him. I was so sure I could help Nina, but I'd given Bernard one more opportunity to knock the props out from under me. I should have expected it.

Talking to him had called up memories I wanted to forget— the day he asked for a divorce. How angry and mortified and scared I'd been. As he had calmly explained to me, as though addressing a jury, how he had fallen in love with Pamela in spite of his determination not to, I had listened, equally dispassionate, at least on the outside. Inside, my stomach felt like molten lava and my lungs couldn't take in enough air. I thought I would surely pass out if not outright die on the spot, but it didn't happen. I wanted to pound on him with my fists and kick him, but I was too numb to move. All I could do was follow his revelation with one of my own: the dates and places of their assignations. It rolled off my tongue as though it had been prerecorded, and all I did was press the right button. And it had the appropriate effect: he was speechless. Didn't that prove I could investigate things? I thought I'd done a masterful job of finding out all about Pamela without Bernard suspecting a thing. But in that case it gave me so little comfort. Why had I kept deluding myself that he'd come back to me? Desperation is not a pretty trait.

How did I feel about him now? Usually I tried not to think about him. Why scratch open an old wound and make it bleed again? The two or three times I ran into him, our exchanges had been brief and impersonal.

I realized that the past year had softened the edges of my pain. It was not gone, but time had blunted it. I came to the conclusion recently that I was in a whole new phase of my life, and I damn well better make the most of it. Though my self image had been badly damaged, it was healing nicely, and I knew I was capable of more than I'd ever dreamed of. I was never going to make big bucks, but it delighted me to be able to make my own decisions, follow my own path. Maybe I could find some way to help Nina, even if Bernard wouldn't let me work with him.

Chapter five

The next morning I asked Logan if I could take some time off. I had yet to take a vacation since I couldn't afford to go anywhere. Several weeks earlier Nina had suggested that we spend a few days in Charleston at her expense. I didn't mind having her pay for dinner occasionally, but I wasn't going to let her do anything that extravagant, so I made up a story about not being able to get away from work. The truth was Logan said I could take time off whenever I wanted it.

"You don't mind if I leave at lunchtime?" I was drinking a cup of coffee and eating one of the Krispy Kremes that Logan had brought in. I'd tried to tell him several times that my willpower never stood up against the sight of those donuts, but he persisted in bringing some in at least once a week. His sweet tooth was even worse than mine.

"That should be okay. Lucy said she'd be glad to help out any time to pick up a few extra bucks." Lucy, who preceded me, had reluctantly retired at 75. "You taking a trip?"

"No. You know the Sellars death that was called in yesterday? His wife's been arrested for his murder. She's a good friend of mine."

"No joke! I saw that on TV last night. That was a pretty wild story, wasn't it? Never did understand why they arrested her. What do you know about it?" He picked up his second donut and took a bite.

"The police aren't saying for now. Anyway, I want to take a few days to see how I can help. Try to cheer her up at least. I feel so sorry for her."

"You know we can't process the claim till we see what the outcome is on this."

"I understand." I knew that if Nina were convicted, she'd never see a dime of the insurance.

"Take as long as you want. Lucy always bakes me brownies when she comes in." He rubbed his belly in anticipation. Logan, who was sixty-one, somehow managed to keep his waistline within a few inches of a boyish physique. He loved to golf, and I guess he walked the calories off over the golf course on the weekends. His auburn hair was now gray at the temples, and he recently had begun to let it curl over the edge of his collar which made him look more than ever like a college professor. His hazel eyes twinkled behind bifocals, hinting at the ready laugh that would burst forth at the slightest provocation.

I assumed the reference to brownies was a hint. "Better get your fill of brownies off Lucy, 'cause I don't do windows or bake."

"As long as you can do the computer work, that's fine with me. Bless Lucy. She bakes a mean brownie, but she hated the computer and never really got the hang of it. So your job's in no jeopardy. But if you want to take off every now and then so I can have my brownie fix, that's okay too."

I went home for lunch, then called the county jail to see if I could visit Nina. The answer was no. Only relatives were allowed.

The only relative nearby, other than Bernard who was a first cousin once removed, was a sister who lived in Reidsville, a town north of Greensboro. I had never met her since the sisters were not close. Nina was a junior in high school when Michelle was born and had left to go to UCLA when she was two. Nina had rarely returned to the area until her recent move back, so the sisters were practically strangers. There were five children in the family, but the rest of the siblings lived in far-flung places, and their father, Frank, had moved to Wisconsin when their mother died about five years ago.

But a relative is a relative. I hoped that Michelle might have already visited Nina or could be convinced to do so. Then I could at least get second-hand information on how she was doing. I got her number through information and called to ask if I might visit her. I had to explain to her who I was since I had been married to the family expatriate.

"Yes, sure, come on up," Michelle said. "You were lucky to catch me on my day off."

I drove north on Route 29 toward Reidsville which had taken a hit when the tobacco and textile manufacturers closed. At one time, Greensboro, like much of the region, had some of the least expensive housing in the country. But in the last decade many high tech industries had located there, and it had grown rapidly, bringing in college-educated young people who could afford fine homes and high-rent apartments. The market rapidly adjusted to their pocketbooks, sending lower-paid people scurrying to find affordable housing, which usually meant moving to one of the small satellite towns that ringed Greensboro.

It was a twenty-nine mile drive over gently rolling countryside. I hadn't been over this route in years because the other major metropolitan areas of the state lie to the east and west over superhighways. Only a few small towns are scattered in the open countryside up this way and there was little incentive to go there. I passed fields of tobacco plants with their lower leaves picked that made them look like miniature palm trees. Since the tobacco industry was in decline, there were fewer of these now. Tobacco farmers were turning to other crops, including grapes for wine. Adjacent to the open fields, kudzu had turned wooded lots into ghostly landscapes by draping every bush and tree, transforming them into green specters. A profusion of yellow "ditch daisies" brightened the edges of the road.

When I arrived in Reidsville, I found that a number of the buildings in downtown were vacant. Evidently it was still struggling to revitalize its center as so many other small towns were trying to do. I found Park Street where Michelle lived. Here the houses were mid-century little square brick boxes. Two blocks down on the right I found 205 E. Park, her address. The house was shaded by a large pin oak, and the lot's perimeter was defined by towering red tip hedges. Scraggly nandina bushes struggled to thrive in the red clay around the foundation. I pulled my car slowly and carefully into the rutted gravel driveway behind an old white Chevy Suburban.

I knocked on the screen door, peering into the dark interior. A woman came from the back of the house, wiping her hands on a dish towel. She was several inches taller than Nina and had decidedly more of a figure. She wore a white tee shirt and black slacks, and her hair was a medium brown worn in a ponytail down her back. The only family resemblance at all was in the down-sloped eyes.

"Tommi?" she asked as she opened the screen. "Hi, I'm Michelle." She made a gesture toward her left. "Come in and 'scuse the dump."

I couldn't think how to respond to that graciously, so I said, "Nice to meet you, Michelle. I guess you could say we're almost related since my ex-husband is your first cousin once removed." She attempted a hearty laugh which was not altogether successful. "You realize," I continued, "I had to memorize that part. Never could get the hang of that once or twice removed stuff. I'm surprised we never met, though."

I entered the house directly into a small living room furnished in older pieces, more early attic than antique. A plain brown sofa, two chairs covered in clashing prints, a squat oak coffee table and mismatched end tables filled up the space. Looking like a lawn in desperate need of fertilizer, the chartreuse shag carpet clashed with everything else, and magazines and newspapers littered the tables. The layer of dust over everything was the only common denominator in the room.

"Since Dad and Cousin Bernard haven't spoken in years, it's not really surprising. I was almost grown before I even learned of his existence," Michelle said.

"Do you happen to know what that's all about?"

"Haven't a clue. We just were told that they didn't speak, and no one ever discussed it."

I hadn't expected to learn anything on that subject, but it didn't hurt to try.

"Have a seat," Michelle said, motioning toward the sofa. She then flopped gracelessly in one of the chairs and crossed her leg so that her ankle rested on her other knee. From her posture, I guessed she'd been the tomboy in the family. She seemed all awkward elbows and knees.

"I wondered if you'd seen or talked to Nina or were planning to," I asked. "I tried to see her this morning, but they told me only relatives were allowed at the jail."

"Well, no." Michelle looked unperturbed over her sister's plight. "I figured she'd be out on bail soon, then I could give her a call or something." She played with a strand of hair that had escaped the rubber band and hung limply down her neck, all curl removed by her relentless twisting of it.

"I'm really concerned about her," I said. "I'd even be glad to drive you to the jail to visit her so you could tell me how she's doing."

"I'm sure she's doing okay. You know they always treat rich people differently. She's probably getting the royal treatment. Anyway, she'll probably be out sooner than we could get over there." She picked up a pack of cigarettes from a table and lit up, blowing smoke lazily at the ceiling.

I was appalled at her lack of concern and could see she would not be much of an ally. It was apparent that she was not motivated to rush to Nina's aid. But even more surprising, she didn't even mention Cap's death. It was like a non-event as far as she was concerned. I'd hoped she would talk about him because all I knew was what Nina had told me. Michelle could have a different picture of him altogether.

"Tell me what you know about Cap. Did you like him?" I asked. I was determined to get some kind of a reaction out of her. It angered me that she would be so apathetic about her sister's predicament.

Michelle shrugged. "I barely knew him. I guess you know Nina and I didn't see much of each other. I was a baby when she left home, so we never had a chance to become close. I've been to their house in Oak Ridge two or three times since they moved back, but that's about it. So I really can't judge him. I knew he had a drinking problem, though I guess he must have been pretty smart to make all that money and everything."

"Had you heard that Cap was having an affair?"

"No kidding! That's news to me. She never told me much at all about her private life. Nina and I would talk about movies and TV programs, stuff like that. I guess she was probably embarrassed all to hell over that and didn't want anyone to know about it."

"She was devastated by it as you can imagine. But she told me she was still crazy about him. And determined to hang onto him. As far as that was concerned, she thought things had turned around in her marriage and had the feeling that he was losing interest in the other woman."

Michelle pursed her lips and looked at me thoughtfully for a couple of minutes. "This sounds ugly since she is my sister. But sometimes I wondered if it wasn't the money and the lifestyle that she loved the most. That girl could shop till she dropped. She loved to flaunt her expensive clothes and stuff."

"That isn't the impression that I got," I countered. "She said Cap was the one who wanted the huge house and the fancy stuff and the 'society' friends."

Michelle lifted her eyebrows meaningfully but said nothing. Just then a raucous sound came from the rear of the house, and Michelle jumped up. "That's my oven timer. Come on out to the kitchen. I baked one of those frozen pies for you. Let's have a piece and some coffee."

The kitchen was quite small with an apartment-size stove and refrigerator, minimum counter space, and printed pressed-board cupboards. Fish plaques on the green walls made me feel like I was immersed in a fish tank.

We sat at a drop-leaf maple table beside a window that overlooked a small backyard. Eight-foot-high red tips surrounded the lot and the kitchen door opened onto a concrete patio with a three-legged barbecue grill and a couple of plastic lawn chairs. Beyond that was a small garden patch where three tomato plants vied for space with squash vines and weeds.

Michelle served me a piece of apple pie and a cup of coffee. The pie crust had all the consistency and flavor of very stale soda crackers. The apples weren't quite thawed.

"Michelle, do you know the names of any of the people Cap liked to socialize with in Greensboro? Nina never mentioned any names to me."

Michelle rubbed her right ear lobe as she contemplated her answer. "They're way out of my league. If she mentioned names, they wouldn't have meant anything to me. Only thing I can think of is to look up old society columns in the local newspaper. They were in it all the time. The names you want would be there too. Why do you want to know about them?"

"I was toying with the idea of talking to some of them. Maybe they'd know of someone who had a grudge against Cap. A jealous husband maybe. I understand he could be quite a flirt."

"You don't think Nina is guilty then."

"Of course I don't! She could never have done anything like that." I wanted to take Michelle and shake her. Her own flesh and blood!

"I sure hope you're right."

I was shocked that Michelle could have doubts about her own sister, but under the circumstances, I realized it wasn't too surprising. They seemed to have little, if anything, in common, and absolutely no sense of sisterly empathy. And an underlying theme of jealousy permeated everything that Michelle said.

"Do you think your brothers and other sister will be coming to the funeral?" I asked. Maybe they could have more insight into Nina's marriage than Michelle did.

"Bill and Claudia are coming, but Ron can't make it. That reminds me, I have something I want to show you." Michelle got up and went into the living room.

I watched a robin hopping about the yard pecking fruitlessly for worms. I wished I could surreptitiously give him the rest of my pie. It was awful.

In a few minutes Michelle returned with an eight-by-ten photo that she placed on the table beside my plate. "Here's a picture of our family when we were growing up," she said. "Since Bernard kept you away from us, I thought you might like to see it." It was a Christmas photo with a decorated tree in the background. Two adults, looking to be in their late thirties or early forties, were surrounded by five children, all brightly smiling and each of the younger ones was holding a Christmas toy.

"Here I am," she pointed to a toddler in front who was clutching a doll. "And here's Nina." Nina was a dark-haired, attractive teenager, standing beside her father. "This was her senior year in high school. The next year she went to California. This is Bill, Claudia, and Ron," she pointed out each of her siblings. They all were dark haired, slender, and their most notable feature was their eyes. They all resembled their mother in that respect. She was a handsome woman, and Nina was almost a carbon copy of her. The boys tended to look more like their father. Claudia had a mixture of features from both parents. All in all it was an attractive family. I felt cheated I had not known them at that time.

"Nice picture. I suppose I'll never have much chance to get to know Ron or Bill or Claudia since they live so far away. But maybe you and I can get together occasionally." It was difficult to sound sincere after her indifference to Nina's situation, but I was trying my best to be polite. Since Nina and I had become so close, I felt I owed Michelle a gesture of friendship. But Michelle didn't strike the same chord as Nina had, and it had nothing to do with vastly different lifestyles. Michelle came across as coarse, with a bit of an attitude problem. Not that she'd been rude or anything, but her lack of concern over Nina indicated self centeredness. It was probably because Michelle was the baby of the family, a little spoiled. Now I understood why Nina hadn't tried to strengthen her relationship with her baby sister.

"Well, I do work in Greensboro, you know, so maybe we can have lunch one day or go to a movie some evening," Michelle replied unenthusiastically. I guess the feeling of disinterest was mutual.

I had to force myself to look pleased. "Oh, where do you work?"

"In the linen department at Belk's. Tuesday nights I bowl, but I'm free other nights."

"That would be nice; we'll have to do that," I said, hoping my lack of sincerity wasn't too obvious. "How long have you lived in Reidsville?"

"A couple of years. After my divorce, I decided I wanted to change everything. So I changed my name back to Poag and moved up here. I like this little town. I don't feel like I have to compete with anybody in this place."

That seemed to sum up the sisters' relationship: competition. At least from Michelle's viewpoint.

I pushed back my chair. "Well, I need to be off now," I said, taking my plate to the sink. "Thanks for seeing me. And I guess we'll see each other again at the funeral."

"I'll be there," Michelle said. "I'm picking up Bill and Claudia at the airport, and we'll go directly to the church."

As I drove back to Greensboro, I reflected on Nina and Michelle. Since I only had a brother, I'd always been envious of women who had sisters. I knew many who considered their sisters their best friends. How sad there was so little connection between those two. Perhaps if they'd been closer in age, it would have been different. Both time and space had conspired to keep them apart till it was too late. And of course life circumstances played a huge role as well.

Chapter six

By the time I'd gone by the grocery store and picked up enough TV dinners and cat food to last for several days, it was time for the local news. Again Nina was the lead story, but at least it was good news this time: Bernard had posted bail, and the video showed him leading her down the courthouse steps as she tried not to be intimidated by the flashing cameras poked within inches of her face. She was putting on a brave front, but I could tell from the tension around her mouth that she was on the verge of crying. She'd been released earlier in the afternoon, so she should be home by now. Michelle had been right that Nina would not linger in jail.

I picked up the phone and dialed Nina's number in Oak Ridge, but got a busy signal. I tried to call her repeatedly for the next hour but couldn't get through. Each time I felt more frustrated. Finally I gave up and decided to drive out to Nina's house.

It was nearly eight o'clock when I arrived, and there was a strange car in front, a silvery gray Lexus. I knocked on the door, and when Nina opened it, she fell crying into my arms. I held her, smoothing her hair, whispering in her ear, "It's okay. It's okay."

Finally she pulled back. "Thanks for coming, Tommi. You've no idea how good you look to me." She was wiping her cheeks with the sleeve of a soft blue sweater that matched the blue in her plaid slacks. "Come on in. Bernard's here." She looked at me with a question in her eyes as if afraid I might turn around and leave.

Bernard was the last person I wanted to see. But if I was going to be of any support to Nina, I had to accept the fact he was her lawyer and would be around a lot. And I should be adult enough not to let it bother me. "So he got himself a Lexus, did he?" I said as I stepped into the foyer, trying for a jovial tone. "He drove a Chevy when he was married to me."

Nina led me to the family room where Bernard was seated on a sofa drinking Perrier. He rose, his greeting perfunctory, as if this were a daily occurrence that needed no amenities instead of the first time we'd seen each other in months. He hadn't changed dramatically; but then it had only been a year since we'd split. I sometimes entertained visions of him wasting away from remorse. What idiocy. He still held himself erect as though his long-ago military training had permanently stiffened his spine. His long and narrow face was unsmiling, and his dark hair only slightly more gray. But he seemed even more somber than usual, perhaps because for once he was dealing with a case he could relate to personally. His usual clients, whose interests lay solely in business dealings, never touched his soul. I wondered if Bernard might have been a different sort of man if his work had been more emotionally satisfying, or at least had engaged his feelings one way or another.

Nina offered me my choice of a drink, and I asked for a beer. Calories be damned. She got each of us a Coors out of the refrigerator, then the two of us settled onto a sofa that faced Bernard's.

"I hope I'm not interrupting anything," I said. "I tried calling you for an hour but the line was always busy. So I decided to come on out."

"Not at all," Nina said. "Bernard brought me home, and we were discussing what happens next. I'm so glad you came. I finally took the damn phone off the hook. It was reporters and TV people mostly. They won't leave me alone. Paparazzi!" She looked disgusted.

I felt constrained by the fact Bernard was there. I wanted to ask Nina all about her ordeal but was afraid Bernard would object. "I had to come tell you how terrible I feel about what you've been through. I'm so very sorry about Cap. And as if that wasn't enough, then to have to go through this other...mess." I put my arm around her shoulder and hugged her.

Nina's face contorted as if she were about to break down again, but then she shuddered and regained her composure. "It was a nightmare, Tommi, pure and simple." She looked at Bernard. "I can tell her what happened, can't I?"

He looked positively gruff. "I suppose so. But Tommi's the exception, you understand. I know you two are close, and I'm sure you'd confide in her sooner or later." Then he turned to me. "But don't you go getting any bright ideas about getting involved in this case."

I only spread out my arms and shrugged, as if of course I'd do what he asked. But he didn't get it in writing. He could never come back and claim I'd made a verbal agreement either. I doubt that I fooled him, but he didn't say anything more. He just gave me his baleful stare.

Nina leaned forward and patted Bernard's hand. "Thanks. I need someone to lean on. Not that you aren't there for me, Bernard, but you're always so busy. I can cry on Tommi's shoulder whenever I get the urge." She turned to me and smiled. "I guess that sounds pretty presumptuous, but I know Logan doesn't mind if I call you now and then at work. He's pretty laid back from what I've seen of him."

"That's true," I said, "but I've asked for a few days off anyway, just in case there's anything I can do for you. Help with the arrangements. Call relatives. Whatever you need."

"Bernard made the funeral arrangements while I was incarcerated and called everyone. He wanted to take the burden off of me."

"Well, anything at all, Nina. I'll do whatever you ask."

"God, but you're a good friend. And if I ever needed one more than now..." Nina readjusted the sofa pillows behind her back so she was facing me, and clutched one to her breast, hugging it to herself as if trying to hold herself together. "I'm going to tell you the whole story. And I guess the best place to start is at the beginning. As you know, Cap had only been home a couple of days. And he couldn't wait to get together with the crowd in Greensboro. So we went with a bunch of people to the N Club, that nightclub on Elm Street, and Cap got smashed as usual. I usually won't argue with him in public, but he was being so damned obstinate, we finally got into a near shouting match."

"What were you arguing about?"

"Driving the car. He has...had...this stupid macho thing about driving. When he was sober, he admitted he shouldn't drive when he was drunk. But when he'd had too many, all reasoning went out the window, and he insisted it was the man's place to drive the woman home. No matter what. I'd been in a couple of fender benders with him when he was drinking...I think I told you about one on the California freeway...and I was scared to death. So I made up my mind that I'd drive, no matter how much he argued with me."

"So you were behind the wheel when this...accident happened?"

"That was no accident. It was deliberate. And if he'd been in the driver's seat, he'd be just as dead, but I wouldn't be blamed for it." Her face clouded up, and she stifled a sob.

I figured they might both be dead if he'd been driving, smashed against a tree somewhere.

Nina got herself under control and continued. "I felt really bad about the argument when he'd just gotten back from California. I hadn't seen him in months, and I was so anxious to patch things up. So before coming home, I took him to Lake Brandt since that's our very favorite place in Greensboro. I told you how much he loved boating, that's how he got his nickname, and when he was in town we'd putz around in our little cabin cruiser on weekends. I never took you out, Tommi, because I've never learned how to drive it. It was his toy, and I was always afraid I'd do something to mess it up. So I wasn't planning to go out in the boat, but I thought just being by the lake might calm him down, and we could talk things out in a reasonable way."

"Did it work? Did he chill out?"

Nina chewed her lower lip trying to keep her voice even. "I never found out. I'd pulled onto the boat ramp to get close to the water. I wanted to see the moonlight reflected on its surface. We'd just gotten there...I hadn't even turned off the engine or unbuckled my seat belt yet...when something came up behind us. Before I knew what was happening...," Nina paused and took a deep breath, "it pushed our car down the ramp into the lake." She closed her eyes and rubbed the worried crease between her brows with her forefinger. Her voice grew softer now. "I got out through the window, but Cap didn't make it. Oh, God," her voice broke, "I feel so guilty. I'd insisted he wear his seatbelt. Can you believe that? I'm such a safety freak I made him put it on. And that's what killed him because I couldn't get it off, and he was too drunk to save himself."

"It just came out of nowhere? The car?"

"Yes, I have nightmares about it. When they first touched the bumper, I couldn't figure out what it was...no headlights or anything. Our car started moving, and I stomped on the brake...," she hugged the pillow even more tightly to her chest, "but I couldn't stop it. It just kept going no matter what I did. I was panicky. I couldn't think what to do except hold that brake down. It was horrible, horrible...," She stopped talking for a minute and stared down at the pillow. Finally she looked up at me and continued. "I started screaming, and Cap looked at me like I'd lost my mind. He didn't understand what was going on. I got my seat belt off before we hit the water, and started to work on Cap's just as we started to sink. Cap was a big man, and when water started coming in the car, he was like a crazy man trying to get out of the seat. I guess his flailing about and pulling against the belt kept me from getting it undone. By that time I was frantic, too, because I can't swim. Finally I rolled down my window so I could get out. I knew then that I couldn't save him, and I might not be able to save myself either. I managed to push myself out of the window and dog paddle back to the edge of the lake. Not far...maybe fifteen feet. It wasn't too deep there, just enough so that the top of the car was under water. My side anyway. There was an air pocket on Cap's side, so they got him breathing again when the emergency squad came, but he died in the hospital." She stopped and got a handkerchief from her pocket and dabbed at the tears that had begun to run down her cheeks.

"Did you see the other car at all?" I asked. Hearing the details of her ordeal made me want to gather her in my arms and let both of us cry our hearts out. But that would do her no good. She needed me to be strong for her.

"No. As I said, there were no headlights, so when I looked in the mirror, all I could see was a dark shape. Then all I could think about was keeping us from being shoved into the water, and getting out of the car, so I never looked a second time."

"What about when you got back to shore?"

"They were gone. They must have taken off immediately because there was no one in sight." She picked up a second pillow to hug as the experience became more and more difficult to relive.

"Do you have any idea why someone would do a thing like that?" I had never heard of anything so bizarre, but Nina wouldn't make up a story like that.

Nina shook her head forlornly. "Only thing I can think of it must have been some kids' idea of a cheap thrill. And when the car went all the way in the water, they panicked and left."

"But why do the police think *you* did it?"

Nina gestured toward Bernard in frustration. "You explain it. It's so ridiculous I can't even talk about it." She buried her chin in a pillow and closed her eyes.

"There's supposedly an eyewitness," Bernard said, "some kid who claims he was in the picnic area near the boat ramp. Went there after his shift at McDonald's. Says he saw Nina stop the car on the ramp, get out, and push it into the lake. Then she jumped in the water so she'd be wet when she went to get help."

"And the cops believe this joker?" I asked in disbelief. It was inconceivable that Nina would have the strength for pushing a heavy car. Besides, it was simply unthinkable she'd do anything like that at all.

"Apparently they've checked him out, and he's clean. No record. Does well in school and so on," said Bernard. "Nothing to make them be suspicious of his account." I suppose it was his training as a lawyer that he could say that without a trace of emotion. Maybe it was a good thing I hadn't finished law school. I could never be dispassionate enough.

Tears were inching down Nina's cheek now. "This jerk, this Colin Somebody-or-Other is probably one of the kids who pushed us in. Or is a friend of theirs. They must have gotten scared the cops would find them out, so they had to make up this horrible story to put the blame on me."

"Weren't there any marks on your car that would prove you were pushed?"

"They say there was some minor damage to the bumper, but there were other banged-up places too. So the police figured it was old damage. Like I told you, Cap had some fender benders, and he didn't always get them fixed. He took care of his car, and I took care of mine. I never could understand how he could spend so much money on a fancy automobile, and not keep it up. He usually claimed he was too busy to deal with it. If he didn't mind driving around in a dented car, I wasn't going to worry about it. I can see now that was a big mistake."

"Weren't there tire marks? If you were holding down the brakes, it would have left rubber behind. That's a concrete ramp isn't it?"

"There were some. But the police theorize I made them by slamming on my brakes before I pushed it into the water...to substantiate my story."

Just then a lilting chime interrupted our conversation. I recognized it as the front door bell.

Nina glanced at her watch. "It's nine-thirty. I wonder who that could be. I hope it isn't another damn reporter."

"I'll get rid of them," I said. My only role in helping Nina at this point amounted to getting rid of pesky newsmen.

I turned on the outside light to illuminate the porch area and opened the door to reveal a tall, thin man dressed in a rumpled plaid sport coat, white shirt unbuttoned at the collar, and wrinkled gray slacks. He was about my age, but there was no sign of gray in his hair.

"Can I help you?" I asked, wondering if this could be a neighbor here to offer condolences.

"Is Nina here? I'm her father, Frank Poag."

It was then I noticed the small suitcase that sat beside him on the porch.

Chapter
seven

So this was the mysterious Frank Poag. He looked weary and frazzled and pretty ordinary. I wasn't sure what I'd expected. The only thing he and Bernard had in common was the same hairline, a gentle widow's peak that receded slightly on either side. He did not have Bernard's erect bearing nor his authoritative demeanor. At least not now.

"Come on in," I said, stepping aside. "I'm Tommi Poag, Bernard's former wife."

He stepped into the hallway and set the suitcase beside the cherry console table, seeming to size me up as he removed his jacket and slung it over his arm. "So you're Tommi." He studied my face, but he did not smile. He looked too world weary for that. He finally nodded his head once. "About time we met," he said extending his hand for a shake. "Where's Nina? Has she been released?"

"She's back in the family room with Bernard. They've been talking over strategy for her case." I wondered what his reaction would be and didn't have to wait long to find out.

"God damn!" His voice exploded in an angry outcry. He strode quickly down the hall to the kitchen, following the sounds of voices at the rear of the house. I was right behind him.

As he entered the family room, both Nina and Bernard stood up, surprise registering on their faces.

"Dad!" Nina rushed to him and threw her arms around his neck. Then she began to sob into his shoulder. He held her tenderly and kissed the top of her head.

"Don't cry, honey. I'm here to help you," He pleaded, stroking her hair as he held her. It was obvious that father and daughter were very close.

At last she calmed down and let him go. Frank stepped back and looked at Bernard, his mouth set in a thin, determined line, his eyes reflecting his anger.

"Hello, Bernard," he said finally, in a voice cold with contempt.

Bernard gave a curt nod, saying nothing, his jaw clenched tight as if trying to keep words from spilling out that he'd regret.

"Come on," said Nina, "let's all sit down and try to be civil."

Bernard, Nina and I sat back down on the couches, but Frank didn't move. He stared at Nina, anger and determination creating a look of such intransigence that he resembled his detested cousin. "Nina, I want you to fire Bernard. Don't you realize he does nothing but write wills? He cannot help you." Though he spoke softly, barely restrained emotion made his voice brittle.

Nina looked at him in shock. "But, Daddy, we discussed this, and you know I have complete confidence in him. Besides he does know criminal law. Remember when he worked in the Public Defender's office? What about that case he won that got so much attention?"

Frank hit the corner of an end table so hard with his fist it made the lamp wobble, causing Nina to grab it to keep it from falling. "Godammit, this is too serious for you to be taking chances with your life," he said. "It's been years since he did that. You've got to do what's best for you."

Bernard, scowling, sat up straighter to glower at Frank. "Now Frank, I was damn good when I worked for the P.D. I won more cases than anyone else in the department. You don't lose those skills; they're always there. I'm as good a defense lawyer as she could get."

Frank's face reddened with contempt. "You, Bernard, are a piece of work. I want you the hell off this case."

There was a moment of complete silence, and the tension in the air was almost electric.

Nina finally spoke. "Dad, it's my life we're talking about here, and I'm an adult. And if I chose Bernard for my lawyer, then that's the way it's going to be. I'm right on the ragged edge now, and I can't take you two men carrying on your grudge match here. This is neither the time nor the place." She burst into the heaviest crying I'd seen from her yet. Knowing I couldn't console her, I sat there helplessly. In fact, I felt so uncomfortable in the middle of all this, I wanted to run home and forget the whole thing. I knew now what it was like to be in the crossfire of a war that I had nothing to do with.

Frank shook his head wearily, as though unable to accept her rejection of his advice. "I can't believe you could be so stubborn, Nina. I only want what is best for you."

"Then quit opposing me, Dad. For God's sake, give me credit for some intelligence. I asked for Bernard, and I'm going to stick with him. Period. End of discussion." She stood up and pulled a tissue from a pocket and blew her nose. "I'm going upstairs now. I've had all I can take for one day."

She took my hand and gave it a squeeze whispering, "I'll talk to you later. Thanks for coming." And then she left the room.

Frank looked stricken. He rubbed his temples with both hands, closing his eyes against fatigue and despair. Finally he said to me, "Do you know where I can find a phone book to call a taxi? If anybody needs me or if Nina changes her mind, I'm staying at the Marriott on Greene Street in Greensboro."

"I'm going back to town if you want to ride with me," I said, not relishing the idea of taking him, but wanting to do it for Nina's sake. I needed to get him out of there before any more arguments began. "I don't think there are any taxis in Oak Ridge so you'd have to wait for one to come all the way out from Greensboro."

"If you wouldn't mind." He had lost his bluster and spoke quietly.

I did mind, but I kept my mouth shut.

Before we left, I ran upstairs to make sure Nina was all right. She was lying face down on her bed, her arm tucked under her head.

"Are you okay? Do you want me to spend the night with you?" If she did, getting Frank out of there was going to be a problem. I was sure that Bernard would not offer him a ride. And he wouldn't accept it if he did.

Nina sat up and gave me a wan smile. "No, I'll be fine. Honest. I really need some time alone. Won't you sit with us at the funeral tomorrow, Tommi? I think of you as family."

"Of course, Nina. I'll be there. Now you get some sleep."

Chapter *eight*

Neither Frank nor I spoke till we were well on our way back to Greensboro. I was angry with him for upsetting Nina, even though I understood his reservations about Bernard. He had just not handled the situation well.

Finally Frank said, "I guess you think I'm a real hothead."

I sighed. "Well...you said it. I didn't."

"I'm worried as hell about Nina. All I want is what's best for her. I can't believe that SOB Bernard is what's best. I don't know what's got into her. She was never this stubborn before."

"First of all, being in such a traumatic situation is bound to have its effect on her. And besides that, in the few months I've known her, I've sensed a change," I said. I wanted him to understand where she was coming from. "I think when her marriage was threatened, she dug in her heels and made up her mind not to sit back and let herself become a victim. She decided to take charge of her life. I think that's what's happened here."

"But why *Bernard*, for Christ's sake?" I couldn't see his features in the dark car, but I could tell he was getting all riled up again. Was this the normal Frank? I sure hoped not.

"She probably didn't tell you, knowing what your reaction would be, but they've become quite close since she moved back here. He helped them get settled in, and it's developed into a genuine friendship."

"That's inconceivable."

I was fast losing my patience. "I don't see what's inconceivable about it. Although he's far from my favorite person, as you might imagine, he's been very nice to her. And since you refuse to tell her what your feud's all about, why shouldn't she? Frankly you two men act like a couple of immature adolescents." I shocked myself that I'd said that, but I was fed up with the whole stupid imbroglio. "You two need to get a life."

Frank said nothing for several minutes. Finally he said, "Their friendship must be pretty awkward for you." He had no intention, apparently, of explaining their hatred of each other.

I had calmed down a little after unloading my frustration. "Nina has been very careful to keep us separate. She doesn't talk about him around me, and Bernard wasn't even aware we'd become close. Nina is usually very tuned in to people's feelings. I'm a little surprised she wasn't more willing to listen to you, but it has to be this independence thing she's developed–being her own person. Also, although I hate to admit it, Bernard probably *can* do a good job for her. He was terrific in the Public Defender's office when he was there. The only thing that bothered me was his attitude toward the people he was defending. He had no respect for them, really didn't give a damn about them, just wanted another notch on his belt. With Nina, of course, that won't be the case. He'll give it everything he's got."

"I'm not sure that's enough. But I hope to God you're right."

I realized I'd been saying these things mainly to allay Frank's fears. I wasn't totally convinced myself that Bernard *could* do the best job. I felt he would try to do his best, that for once his heart was in it. But had it been too long since he'd been involved in criminal law?

"How do you think he plans to prove she didn't do it?" Frank asked as we reached Market Street.

"I don't know. You're probably not aware of this, but some kid claims he saw Nina push the car into the lake. So it's not going to be a piece of cake." I was afraid that was an understatement.

"Oh, lord, I didn't know that. Who would say such a thing? And why?" He was getting agitated again. I was kind of sorry I brought it up.

"Nina's convinced some kids pushed their car into the lake in what started out as a joke, and he's lying to save their necks."

"And why would the cops believe him and not Nina?" Frank sounded like he was ready to take on the Greensboro police force single-handedly.

"Neither Bernard nor Nina said if there was any special reason for that. But I have a few hunches of my own. In the first place, Cap recently bought a second life insurance policy. Nina had to send the form to California for his signature. I'm sure that looks suspicious to the police. He already had a million dollar policy and was getting another one for a million with a double indemnity clause. And then they had a loud argument in the nightclub shortly before the accident happened. Evidently a lot of people were witnesses to that."

"What were they arguing about?"

"Who was going to drive. He was very drunk but insisted he would drive her home. Of course she wouldn't let him. Another thing–I don't know how many people know about this woman he was having an affair with. But someone surely mentioned her to the cops. Anyway, all that adds up to several possible motives."

"What woman?"

"Someone named Allison."

"I didn't realize how little she confided in me. Who's Allison?"

"Nobody seems to know."

"Dear God, there are so many strikes against her."

"I'm sure she didn't want to upset you."

"That doesn't sound good at all, does it? What are we going to do, Tommi?" I noticed he said "we" and not "I." Evidently he'd already decided that I was on his side.

"I'm not sure there's much of anything we can do." I wasn't going to tell him about Bernard refusing my offer of help. It would only exacerbate his hatred for him.

"There has to be something. We can't leave it entirely in Bernard's hands. You know, Cap was anything but an angel. God knows who might have wanted him dead. I never understood why Nina stayed with him so long. I wish she'd left the SOB a long time ago."

"You mean you think there might be someone out there who did this deliberately? You don't buy this business of kids doing it as a prank?" I'd had a gut feeling that this might be true, but was glad to have someone else validate my suspicions.

"No, I don't think kids did it. I think it's much more sinister than that. Look, I know how close you and Nina have become. She's talked a lot about you. Why don't you and I work together to see what we can come up with. If I don't do something, I'll go bonkers sitting around twirling my thumbs while Nina is being prosecuted." He was pleading with me now. Frank was going to get involved in this with or without me, I was sure.

"I don't know, Frank. We'd have to do it unofficially and really under the radar because we wouldn't want Bernard or Nina to find out. After that scene tonight, we couldn't ask them for the time of day. They don't want us anywhere near this case."

By now we were in front of the Marriott. Frank hesitated before getting out of the car. "Please think about it, Tommi. I beg of you to give it serious thought."

"I will. I'll consider it." I , of course, wanted to help Nina, and Frank obviously needed some propping up. But how difficult would he be to work with? Would his hatred of Bernard get in the way? I'd really hoped to check things out on my own as much as possible. But maybe two heads would really be better than one. It would be hard to turn him down in spite of the complications involved.

Instead of going directly home, I drove to Lake Brandt, the scene of the crime. It's on the north edge of town, a beautiful small lake that is popular with fishermen and pleasure boat owners. I was so wound up from the events of the evening that I was nowhere ready to go to sleep. And I wanted to see the spot where Nina and Cap had parked that night. I chided myself for acting like the motorists who slow down to gawk at a freeway accident out of morbid curiosity, but promptly excused myself by rationalizing it was only concern for Nina that took me there.

I drove the curving road that led to the lake and stopped close to the boat ramp where Nina said she'd parked. The night was cloudless, and the moonlight reflected on the still water gave a silvery luminescence to the lake and trees that bordered it. Stars flickered brightly in the heavens with that special autumn brilliance. It was hard to envision a tragedy happening there.

I got out of the car and walked over to the ramp. I could see skid marks leading to the water's edge. It made me nauseated to think of the car sinking into the black water, and I felt an urgent need to get away from there. I walked to a nearby picnic table and sat down.

Again I wondered if I should agree to Frank's proposal to work with him. Would we be working *against* Nina's interest since we couldn't tell her what we were doing? Or could we really accomplish something, perhaps discovering facts that Bernard, or whoever worked for him, would not know? Maybe if we were very discreet, we could poke around and come up with evidence that would point the finger of guilt at someone else. I was afraid Frank would be very prickly and difficult to work with, but, after all, the goal here was to help Nina. I guessed I could put up with him for her sake.

It suddenly dawned on me that the so-called "witness" must have been near this very spot when he supposedly saw Nina push the car into the water. *What absolute crap.* Why would anyone make up such a vicious and damning lie? I remembered that there was a McDonald's not far away, and it must be where he was employed. I had to see this guy for myself. If he'd come here after he got off work the night Cap died, that meant he was on the last shift, and he'd probably be there now.

I left the park and drove over to the restaurant at the corner of Battleground and Westridge. Very few people were there. I was surprised since it was almost ten-thirty on a Friday night, and I'd supposed it would be filled with teenagers. They were probably at the high school football games..

I was waited on immediately and ordered a chocolate shake even though the emotional events of the evening had left me with no appetite. It was a rare occasion when chocolate didn't appeal to me.

"Is there a Colin who works here?" I asked,

The young man waiting on me looked surprised. "Yeah, that's me." He was a handsome young man, tall and blonde, clean cut. My heart sank. He could make a very credible looking witness at least. I'd hoped for some scruffy-looking kid who would turn off a jury.

"Uh, is there any chance I could talk to you in private?" I'd really only come to see what he looked like, but now that I'd found him, I couldn't resist talking to him. I was hoping I could get him to retract his statement that he'd given to the police, naive as I was. Hadn't I been persuasive when I talked to people on the crisis line so many years ago?

"I guess so. I'm due for a break in about five minutes. Why don't you sit down and I'll be there shortly." He was all politeness.

I muttered "thanks" and went to the rear of the restaurant where we could have more privacy.

Colin joined me in a few minutes, carrying a Coke for himself.

"Yes, ma'am, how can I help you?" he asked as he sat down.

Though I knew it was unreasonable, the "ma'am" irritated me. He was being polite, but it made me feel a million years old. And it seemed to me it was just an act anyway.

"I'm a friend of Nina Sellars," I said, staring at him pointedly.

"Who?" He looked truly puzzled.

"The woman *you* said pushed her car into the lake." I was trying not to sound testy, but it came out petulant in spite of myself. The thought occurred to me that the police might not appreciate the fact I approached their witness, but, hey, this is a free country, is it not?

"Oh?" His eyes were wary.

"I was just curious about it. How you happened to be there. What you saw."

"How do you know about me? I know my name hasn't been given to the press." He was getting a little testy himself now.

"Her attorney told me about you. He happens to be my former husband. And Mrs. Sellars gave me your name." Well, she'd happened to mention his first name anyway.

He shrugged. "I guess it's okay to talk about it then. You aren't a reporter are you?"

"No, I work in an insurance office."

"And you're a friend of this lady?" He took a sip of his Coke, the epitome of cool.

"Yes, a very good friend." I stared at him in an attempt to intimidate, thinking I needed to work on my imperious glare a bit.

"Well, she's got a screw loose or something." He twirled his finger in the air to illustrate her problem.

"I don't think so." He was some nervy kid.

"Why would she do what she did then?"

"Why don't you tell me about it." I said, ready to shake the complacency out of him.

"Okay." He took another sip of his drink. I wanted him to be sweating or shaking or acting suspicious in some way, but he was perfectly calm. "I get off here at eleven, and I'm always kind of wound up after work. You know, can't get to sleep right away. Last Wednesday it was such a nice night I decided to go to the lake. My girlfriend and I go there a lot so it's kind of a hangout for me. I'd gone into the parking lot and decided to walk along the edge of the lake for a while. Coming back, as I got close to the picnic area, this car pulled in. I mean it kind of raced in and then slammed on the brakes, skidding onto the boat ramp. I'll be honest, I thought it was a couple of kids gonna make out, and I thought it'd be a hoot to wait till they got going hot and heavy and then go up to the car and bang on the trunk. Just to see how they'd react, you know?" He lowered his eyes sheepishly. "I know it sounds kind of dumb now, but my friends think I'm a pretty funny guy."

"Go on," I said, wondering how the world would make out when jokers like this took over.

"As soon as it stopped, a woman got out of the driver's side. I couldn't see anyone else in the car. She rolled the window down, then put it in neutral I think, 'cause she leaned over to do something between the front seats. Then she shut the door and went around behind it and started to push it into the water." He demonstrated by making a pushing motion with both hands.

"What was she wearing?" I asked, thinking I'd nail him on this when he described it wrong.

"I was too far away. Couldn't tell in the dark." He was no dummy, that was for sure.

"How did you know it was a woman then?" Maybe I could trip him up with that.

"Because it came out in the news about this guy drowning and the woman driver getting out, and it happened at the time I was there. So it had to be her."

"You didn't see another car push them into the lake."

"Oh, no, ma'am." He was all earnestness. "She did it herself. That's what I meant about having a screw loose."

"Why didn't you stop her?" That seemed logical to me.

"Stop her?" He looked puzzled. "Would you try to stop somebody doing something crazy like that? I thought she was trying to collect insurance on the car, like maybe it was a lemon or something. When people make their mind up to do weird things, they scare me, you know? I just wanted to stay out of her way. I watched long enough to see her jump in the lake to get herself wet, then get out and start running down the road like she was going for help. That's when I left."

I stared at him for a couple of minutes without comment. Finally I said, "Who's paying you to say this, Colin?"

"What do you mean? Nobody's paying me for anything. You asked what I saw, and I'm telling you." He looked straight in my eyes as he said this. He was remarkably composed. A pathological liar I figured. I could only hope the cops would make him take a lie detector test. But since it is inadmissible, they probably wouldn't.

I just shook my head. "You're really a smooth operator, Colin, I'll give you that. I don't know what your game is, but whatever it is, you're about to ruin a woman's life."

"Hey, look, I'm sorry for her. Maybe she'll get off by pleading she's insane. But I had to tell the truth."

"Yeah, sure. Some truth."

He stood up. "Gotta get back to work now. The cops believe me. I don't know why you can't." He tossed his empty cup into the nearby trash bin and walked back toward the kitchen.

I was sick. I didn't know what was going on, but it looked terrible for Nina.

Chapter nine

Tee woke me up the next morning by walking in circles around me in the bed like Indians surrounding settlers' wagons. Only instead of war cries, plaintive mews. He gets this way when I become distracted and pay little attention to him. Spoiled rotten, that's what he is. But it was useless to stay in bed; he'd just keep it up till he was fed and petted. I got up, fixed myself some breakfast, after appeasing Tee, and gave a passing thought to doing some housework, but soon dismissed it. I was too depressed.

Today was the day of the funeral, and I dreaded it. I was to have met Cap tonight for the first time. Nina had invited me out to the house for dinner, just the three of us. If only I'd gotten to know him, maybe I could get a better fix on what might have happened Wednesday night. I really only knew him through Nina's eyes, and so, of course, I had no objective assessment of him. Frank had mentioned that he wondered why Nina had stayed with him so long. I was going to have to pick his brain when I got the chance. However, he had never lived close to them, so he wouldn't have an intimate knowledge of his son-in-law. And Nina probably didn't want to burden her father with her marital troubles.

I had just finished getting dressed when the phone rang.

"It's Frank Poag." He sounded far more rested and calm this morning.

"Oh, hi." I paced the bedroom as I talked.

"Nina called me first thing this morning. She apologized for last night."

"Whoa, Frank. I think you had more to apologize for than she did."

"I know. I told her that."

Surprise, surprise. Maybe he was a little more sensitive than I thought. "Well, I'm glad you two have made up. She surely needs you on her side."

"She asked me to come stay at the house. Providing I don't mention Bernard."

"I'm glad. I hate for her to be alone out there." This really might be a good solution. At least he could keep her spirits up–as long as they didn't fight about Bernard.

"Right. I'll plan to go back home with her after the funeral. I was wondering in the meantime if you might be free for lunch. I don't think we got off on the right foot yesterday."

I had no other plans, and the funeral wasn't until two o'clock. "Sure. Where do you want me to meet you?"

"How about Bistro 40, right here at the hotel? Around twelve?"

"Sounds good. Then you can ride with me to the funeral." It was going to be at First Presbyterian church right up the street from the Marriott.

"Well, that's fine. But I wasn't doing this so I could get a ride. I wanted another chance to talk to you alone. I haven't yet found out anything about you."

I laughed. "There's not much to know. See you at noon."

Maybe he'd been laying it on a little thick, but I chose my outfit carefully. A teal blue knit suit, a paisley silk scarf around the neck, silver earrings. The suit was dark enough to be appropriate for a funeral, but more becoming than black. I look terribly washed out in black.

I was five minutes early for the lunch date, but Frank was waiting for me in the foyer of the restaurant. When he smiled, his face lit up and was almost handsome. I realized it was the first time I'd seen him smile.

After we studied our menus and ordered–he, a chef salad, and I, a turkey croissant sandwich–he unfolded his napkin and put it on his lap with great deliberation. "I really appreciate your coming," he said with an unexpected shyness. "I feel cheated that I never had the chance to get to know you. All those years you were in our family, and I knew nothing about you except what the relatives told me. And since they're all so closemouthed," he grinned, "that wasn't very much. So I hope I haven't put the kibosh on our relationship by my behavior last night."

"No, no," I waved my hand to dismiss such thoughts, "I know how you felt. Just forget that." I was being kind, because at the time I actually thought he was acting like a horse's ass. But all was forgiven.

"So tell me a little bit about yourself," he said with what appeared to be genuine interest.

I proceeded to describe my current life, my home, my job, and how I'd met Nina.

He, in turn, talked about his wife, Marilyn, and her death from cancer five years before. He was so torn up over it, he said, that when the chance came to transfer to Wisconsin, he took it. "Everything around here reminded me of her constantly. I thought a change of scenery would do me good."

"Did it help?"

"Yes, I'm okay now. Not that I don't miss her; I do. But it isn't that awful debilitating sorrow that overwhelms you at first and makes it so hard to get on with your life."

I knew what he meant. A divorce, after all, hits you like a death. Or maybe worse. He knew that his wife still loved him. There's something healing in that.

"What do you do in Wisconsin?" I wanted to change the subject.

"I work for ACS."

"Oh, good old American Communication Systems. They're more persistent than most trying to get me to switch my phone to them."

Frank smiled again, the first time since talking about his wife. "We are rather aggressive, I must admit. But with so many new companies, you have to be."

While we ate we discussed anything not related to Cap and Nina. Our tastes and preferences seemed to coincide or complement one another more often than conflict. This Frank Poag was quite different from the one I had seen last night. He was calm, funny, literate, and compassionate.

I decided to give him the ultimate test. "Do you like cats?"

"I used to be quite a dog lover," he said, "but I travel a lot on my job, and it got to be too expensive to board them. I missed the companionship, though, so a couple of years ago I got a couple of tabbies. A neighbor's kid feeds them and looks after them when I'm gone."

"Well, you'll have to meet my cat, Tee-nine-cy, that is if he'll come out from under the bed. He gets a little crazy when I have company."

"Tee-nine-cy?"

"That's an old expression that means very small. Well, that's definitely tongue in cheek. He weighs twenty pounds."

Frank got a good laugh from that.

Finally it was time to leave for the funeral. Frank had already checked out of his room, and they were holding his luggage behind the front desk.

The weather refused to take on the appropriate somberness for the occasion. A gorgeous September afternoon greeted us, the sunshine magnifying the colors that heralded the arrival of fall: the magenta shades of the sumac, the dark reds of the dogwood. No low-hanging gray clouds or rumbling thunder. I fought off feelings of cheerfulness; they were entirely out of place.

"Have you given any more thought to our conversation last night?" Frank asked as we drove up Elm Street. "You probably think this lunch was all about buttering you up for this question, but you're wrong. I'd like to be friends with you no matter what you say. I'll respect your opinion on this. If you have misgivings, that's perfectly okay. I understand."

Wow! Would Bernard ever say anything like that? No way. It was always his way or else. Frank was really different. Or he put on a darn good front. "Well, I guess we could give it a shot," I said. "And if we're going to work together, I think I need to confess something."

"What could you possibly have to confess?"

"I looked up the kid who says he saw Nina push the car in the lake."

"Oh my God! I hope you haven't told Bernard about this. Would this be considered tampering with a witness?"

That thought had briefly occurred to me, but I dismissed it immediately. I realized I was pretty naive about this whole business. "I wasn't 'tampering,' Frank. I simply asked him what he saw."

"Which was...?"

"What Bernard told us he said. I'll give him credit. He stuck to his story with a straight face. I know he has to be lying, but the question is why?"

"Regardless of why, it sure doesn't look good for Nina."

Chapter *ten*

We arrived at the church fifteen minutes before the funeral service and already the sanctuary was filling up. Even though Nina and Cap had not lived in the area long, it seemed they had made many friends, or at least Cap had, as Nina felt less than comfortable around them. I wondered, though, if some were simply curiosity seekers who hoped that a movie star might appear.

The First Presbyterian Church is beautiful, inspired by a church in southern France with a brick facade, impressive twin towers, and a huge rose window over the front door. The interior is as impressive as the outside.

I didn't see any famous faces, at least none that were familiar to me, but the mourners were extremely well dressed. I felt almost dowdy compared to them. I did recognize some people from the society pages of our local paper.

Nina was already there, sitting in the second pew with two men and a woman that I didn't recognize. Nina was wearing a plum-colored knit dress with a cowl neck. When she turned to look at us, I saw how pale and sad she appeared. Frank put his hand on my elbow and guided me up the aisle and into the pew next to them.

Nina leaned across the man who sat between us and whispered, "Tommi, I want you to meet Daniel, Cap's brother. And my brother and sister, Claudia and Bill." She gestured toward her right. I nodded acknowledgment and they all nodded back.

In a few minutes Michelle sat down beside Frank. She was wearing a basic black dress that made her face, without makeup, look sallow. Her hair was swept up in a French twist that already was beginning to come apart, leaving strands of hair hanging down her neck. Or maybe that was deliberate, I thought, an attempt to emulate the messy coifs of some movie stars. Probably, though, she just didn't give a damn about her appearance.

Shortly before the service began, Bernard came in and sat beside Michelle. He seemed slightly out of breath. Since he almost always worked on Saturdays when we were married, I assumed he'd probably rushed over from the office, reluctantly pulling himself away from his paperwork. But if it was paperwork that would help Nina, then I was all for it.

The service was brief and impersonal. It was obvious that the minister, some distant relative of Cap's I was told, really didn't know him, but he read the proper passages from the Bible, made reassuring references to the "life everlasting" and asked the congregation to join in singing a couple of hymns. It was a generic funeral, innocuous enough to fit anyone. I felt less than satisfied, as though I'd eaten a meal that left me still hungry.

When it was over, the minister invited everyone to the parlor to meet with relatives. Nina had been emotionally unable to handle the idea of having calling hours prior to the service, in fact she had been in jail part of the day before, and so the post-service reception at the church would serve to accommodate those who wished to offer their condolences. She was simply too overwhelmed by her situation to try to receive them in her home. Claiming urgent business back in the office, Bernard excused himself , but I think he really didn't want to be in the same room with Frank. After he left, Nina led the way out of the sanctuary clinging to Frank's arm, stopping every few minutes to accept murmured words of consolation from others who evidently did not intend to stay. The rest of us, Michelle, Claudia, Daniel and Bill and myself trailed behind them as they made their way slowly to the parlor.

Only about twenty-five people remained for the reception. I wasn't too surprised. Although I'd sat in front of most of the mourners, I'd sensed no undercurrent of genuine grief. Though Cap had been fawned over by the socially prominent clique, I wondered if they really cared about him. Being at that funeral reminded me of watching a television program with the sound off; the actors went through all the motions, but they seemed to be empty gestures.

The large parlor reinforced the impression of a French cathedral from the oriental rugs and tapestries on the walls to the dark, massive furniture. All the relatives formed into a line to greet mourners. In the center of the room a table had been prepared with a lace cloth, a silver coffee service, and plates with dainty sandwiches and cookies.

Before joining the others in the reception line, Frank whispered to me. "Why don't you talk to Cap's lawyer and agent. Nina said they'd both be here. Maybe you can find out something from them. The agent is Morgan Proxmire and Ernie Zaleskie was his lawyer. That tall, skinny guy over there is Morgan. I met him once. I'm going to be tied up for a while with greeting people."

The agent was talking with an elderly woman, so I went to the refreshment table for a cup of coffee and a cookie while I waited for the conversation to end. I glanced around the room and noted that the general atmosphere was anything but somber. It was like any cocktail party I'd ever attended, with lively conversation and occasional laughter. Of course, rarely does everyone mourn openly at such receptions. Tears are allowed to flow in the privacy of one's home or are shed surreptitiously during the service, but "stiff upper lips" are usually the accepted demeanor afterwards. But in the case of Cap's death, I don't think many people outside of his family actually cared. And not all of them mourned him.

The woman who was talking to the agent soon left to stand in line to meet the family, and Morgan came toward the table. As he picked up a cookie, I said, "I'm Tommi Poag, a good friend of Nina's. Any chance I could talk to you for a minute?"

He gestured to some chairs in the corner, away from the crowd, and lowered his lanky body into one of them which was dwarfed by his presence. I wondered if he had been a basketball player, the assumption one usually makes in the presence of anyone so tall, yet so graceful. But I was not going to make a social gaffe by asking him.

I sat next to him since my shoes were beginning to give me a fit. It was the first time in months that I'd worn heels, and they felt like miniature torture chambers.

He took a bite of cookie. "Okay," he said. "Shoot."

I smiled at the coincidence that I'd just been thinking about basketball. "I understand you were Cap's agent."

"True." He nodded and took another bite. It probably took lots of cookies to fill up that long frame. I wondered if all I would get were one-word replies out of him.

How did I begin? "I've become very close to Nina since she moved here. But unfortunately I never met Cap because he's been in California. In fact, this was the day I was to meet him."

He shook his head in disbelief. "The whole thing is unbelievable." He really could talk in sentences.

"Particularly Nina's arrest," I said." I want to do something for her, but I don't know where to begin. Since I didn't know Cap, I'm trying to talk to people who did, to get some kind of a handle on him. What was he like anyway?"

"Well, first of all he was damn talented. He had done very well, but had the potential to demand top dollar. The man had a real knack for the business. He seemed to know exactly what producers were looking for."

"I'd assumed he already commanded the highest pay, living like he did."

"He could have made even more. He just needed to work with the best-known directors. He hadn't quite gotten there yet. But he was on his way."

"Aside from his talent, what kind of a person was he?"

He looked at me for a moment, as if weighing the consequences of what he was about to say, and then continued. "He could be pretty much of a jerk, actually. I used to tell him he'd learned his three "L's" well - lush, lard and lech–he'd been putting on weight from his booze and he liked the ladies. He was different when I first knew him, a really nice guy, but the more successful he became, the more he drank and ran around. Guess he thought that's what 'real' writers were supposed to do. Damned if I know."

"Do you know anything about an Allison? I understand he was pretty serious about her. But she seems to be the mystery woman."

"Yeah, I caught wind of her, but I've no idea who she is. Cap liked to dramatize things. Everything he did had to be larger than life. So you really didn't know how big a deal she was. Had he made her up out of whole cloth just to put Nina on notice that she'd better be the good little wife? I wouldn't have put it past him. Sometimes I felt he confused fiction and real life and didn't know where one ended and the other started." He stood up. "Do you mind if I go back to the refreshment table? You don't get any food on the planes any more, and I came straight here from the airport. I'm starving."

"Please," I gestured. "Go ahead."

He filled up his plate with more cookies, sandwiches and nuts and came back to his chair.

"Okay," he said, munching on a sandwich. "Where were we?"

"It doesn't sound like Cap was your favorite person."

Morgan squirmed in his chair, trying to get comfortable, but it seemed like a too tight shoe. "Actually we started out the best of friends seven years ago. I knew right off he had enormous talent, and I admired him for it. He was one of my first clients."

"What did you do before that?" I had to satisfy my curiosity.

"Played basketball. What else does a giant bastard like me do? But you've only got a few years to do that. I'd really always wanted to be a writer, but I realized early on that I didn't have the talent. So I used my basketball years when I gained a bit of fame for my rebounding as a way to meet people in the writing field. I knew that when I had to quit playing, I wanted to be an agent. But not a sports agent. By that time I was pretty fed up with the dog-eat-dog mentality of the field. And

I figured the next best thing to being a famous writer was to work with some of them."

"You say you started out friends with Cal. What about recently? Did you still consider him a friend?"

He licked his thin lips and ran his hand over his hair. "I was about to drop him. He'd accused me of not passing all the money due him. He said I had sticky fingers which was an out-and-out lie! I never kept a dime that wasn't mine." Morgan's long face was scowling now. And he began fiddling with the ends of his tie. "I think it was the alcohol talking or maybe his growing reputation was going to his head. Or maybe he was just becoming paranoid."

I was amazed he was willing to tell me all of this, but he obviously wanted to get it off his chest. He probably didn't dare say this to anyone in Hollywood, and I was two thousand miles from there and a not connected with the industry. Therefore he could safely vent with me. I looked at him steadily till he finally averted his eyes. "You were going to leave him, or was he going to dump you? I mean if he said you were stealing from him..." I let my voice trail off.

He looked up again, his mouth pursed with irritation. "I'm sure it was an empty threat." So he had been in danger of being fired.

"He knew how much I'd helped his career along. It was a ploy to get the upper hand. I'd always made editorial suggestions on his scripts, and he knew I was almost always right when I proposed changes. But his ego had gotten to the point that he thought he knew it all. He was using this bullshit as a lever to get his way."

"What do you mean by that?"

"He wanted to ask way too much for his work. He wasn't ready for it yet. I told him as his agent I couldn't do it. I'd be the laughingstock and so would he."

"So how would accusing you of theft help him?"

"I had a contract with him. He wanted to break it. It was the only way he could think of to do it."

"Oh, I see. A little blackmail. Sweet guy, huh?"

Morgan brushed crumbs from his pants and set his plate on the table next to him. "And I wasn't the only one sour on him."

"There were others?"

"Some guy named Robert Truesdale was going to sue him for stealing a movie script. He claims Cap took it nearly word for word."

"Where does this Truesdale live?"

"Around here I think. But you'd have to ask Ernie Zaleski, Cap's lawyer. He'd know more about it."

"Is he here?"

Morgan looked around the room and pointed toward the opposite corner. "There he is, talking with the minister."

I felt I'd given the man a hard time, and I'd end the conversation on an upbeat note. "It's been nice meeting you, Morgan. And thanks for talking to me. I hope you didn't mind my asking some tough questions."

"I just want to help Nina. She took a lot of shit off that man. And she sure doesn't deserve what's happening to her. Frankly, I'm not surprised someone was pissed off enough to kill him. But I could never in a million years believe that Nina did it."

He stood as I left, and out of the corner of my eye I saw him head back toward the food.

I headed toward Ernie Zaleski who was now walking toward the refreshment table. I wanted to intercept him before he got there, but I didn't quite make it.

"Mr. Zaleski? I'm Tommi Poag." I thrust out my hand as I approached the attorney. But he had just picked up a small glass plate in one hand and a cup of coffee in the other, and he looked at me in momentary confusion. Finally, he set down the coffee cup just as I withdrew my proffered hand, so we looked at each other sheepishly and laughed.

"You know, it's like when I'm headed into somebody on the sidewalk, and we both keep sidestepping at the same time like we're doing a waltz together. I always feel like such a damn fool," Ernie said. "Next time that happens with a pretty girl, I'm just going to grab her and do the real thing. Care to dance?" He gave me a wicked grin. He was slightly taller than I am with beautiful silvery hair he wore in a blow dry style. He appeared to be about my age, and I was surprised he didn't color his hair since he seemed to be keenly attuned to the latest, and most expensive, style. His Giorgio Armani suit was double breasted, and his pearl gray shirt was starched and ironed to perfection and complemented by an elegant darker gray silk tie. Evidently his hair was supposed to represent "maturity." I had to admit if my hair looked like that, I'd never have a dye job. Instead my natural color is a bad mixture of mousy brown and dingy gray. Hence the dye.

"Do I know you? The name of Poag sounds familiar." He picked up his plate and cup again.

"No, we haven't met. I'm Bernard Poag's former wife. He's Nina's lawyer."

He nodded at me. "That's interesting. The 'ex-' part, I mean. Yes, I've talked a little with Bernard about Nina's case. Shame I can't practice in this state or I'd be glad to help him."

"Could we go sit down?" My high heels were getting worse by the minute..

"Of course. Of course. Lead the way." He gestured with his plate.

I sat down on a brocade-covered sofa in a quiet corner. Ernie sat down beside me, balancing his plate of cookies on one knee and cup of coffee on the other. I was sorry I had chosen the sofa, because he was too close for comfort..

"I never could get the hang of these buffet-type things," he grumbled. "If I let go of anything to try and eat, it'll be upside down on the carpet."

I was sure that anyone in his position could not be as inept as he pretended, but even if it was an act, I found it amusing. Perhaps he thought it broke the ice.

I held up my finger signaling for him to wait and got up and found a small light-weight chair which I placed in front of him. "Put your plates on this."

He set them down gratefully, brushing crumbs from his pant legs and beamed at me. "You don't need a job, do you? My secretary's leaving, and she's the kind who anticipates my every need. She's going to be hard to replace."

Oh, no, I thought, spare me from one of those. "Thanks, anyway, but I already have a job."

"Too bad. You have no idea how interesting and how well paid the job can be." He gave me a wink and salacious smile.

I gave a tight smile back, hoping it would shut him up but not alienate him. I wanted him to answer my questions while forestalling any of his veiled attempts at seduction. "Morgan Proxmire has been telling me about Robert Truesdale, the man who wanted to sue Cap. He said he thought he might live in this area. Is that true?" I didn't explain why I was asking. Since he'd connected me with Bernard, let him think I was working for him. As long as I didn't lie about it, he could assume what he liked.

"Yeah, right. Over in Kernerston...Kerners..."

"Kernersville?"

"That's it. Why do you ask?"

"Oh, I was just kinda curious about him. Do you think he's some kind of crank?"

"Sure. He swears Cap stole his script when he wrote *Astral Express* but he can't prove it. And he has no track record. He's never sold so much as a short story so I doubt very much he has the chops to write such a complicated plot."

"You say doubt. You're not sure, though."

"As sure as I could be about anything. If Cap said he never heard of him, then I believed Cap." He sipped his drink and ate a cookie. I wondered if he and

Morgan had been on the same plane. Ernie didn't seem nearly as hungry. He'd only taken two small cookies.

"How does this man say it happened?" I asked.

"He claims he passed along his script to his aunt who knew Nina somehow. She sent it to them in California and put in a good word for him."

"Why would he want to send it to a screenwriter? Isn't that just asking for trouble?"

"He says he wanted to collaborate with someone well known. He thought his plot idea was very original, but he knew he needed help with some of the finer points. And he thought it was impossible to get a foot in the door in Hollywood since nobody knew him. According to him, he wanted to share the credit with Cap."

"Did you ever speak with his aunt?"

"It wasn't necessary. Truesdale had no proof at all. He didn't register it with the Writers' Guild or copyright it or anything. It's a common thing to have some nut suing for plagiarism in the movie business."

"Would you happen to have his address or phone?"

"Why would you want it? Isn't it rather a moot point now?" He wiped his mouth daintily with his napkin.

I gestured vaguely and shrugged as though it should have been obvious. "You know, leave no stone unturned, as they say. Just doing a little background check." I gave him a smile as if to say we're all in this together. I wanted him to think I was doing undercover work for Bernard. God help me if they compared notes.

"I might have the information back at the hotel in my briefcase."

"I'd appreciate it so much." I got out my billfold and pulled out a business card which I handed to him. Logan had them made up when I first went to work for him. It read "Tommi Poag, Administrative Assistant, Stewardship Life." What a nice euphemism for plain old secretary. It was the first time I'd had an occasion to use one.

Ernie looked it over. "Life insurance? I thought you worked for Bernard."

"There are some very large policies at stake with this case. That made it seem natural for me to help out." I didn't say who I was helping out.

He pulled out his own wallet and stuck it in the bill compartment. "Sure. I'll give you a call later tonight,"

"And you're staying at…?" I didn't feel entirely confident he would do so and wanted to be able to reach him just in case.

He must have thought it was a come on. "The O. Henry Hotel. Better yet," he said, "why don't I bring the information over to your house?"

"Oh, sorry, " I replied, "I've got to wash my hair and do some laundry tonight." Honest to God, I hadn't found it necessary to make up a silly excuse like that since I was in high school.

Chapter *eleven*

The receiving line was breaking up, and I saw Nina heading my way as Ernie Zaleski left.

"We're going to the cemetery now to have the ashes interred. It's a fairly long way, and we couldn't see the point of having everybody follow us over there for a five-minute ceremony, so it'll just be family. And you're included in that designation. Then we're going back to the house. Do you want to ride with us? Someone can bring you back here later to get your car."

"No point in that. I'll follow you."

Frank, his children, and Daniel all rode in the limousine that had been provided by the funeral home. I followed in my Mitsubishi making a strange procession, one large limo, one small van. The cemetery was halfway between Oak Ridge and Greensboro, one of the newer breeds of burying grounds where no marker or stone rose above the level of the carefully nurtured grass. At one time I thought that such memorial gardens were impressive with their rolling, undisturbed lawns until my own parents were buried in one. I always have difficulty finding the graves. And the sea of indestructible artificial flowers posing stiffly row upon row seems maudlin to me. Maybe that's how people identify their loved ones: look for the purple and pink roses in the green basket. At least in an old fashioned cemetery you can get your bearings from the variety of markers and monuments. And there is something about the rows of headstones that appeals to me: a certain dignity, a reminder of the uniqueness of individuals. Even in death one can at least have a distinctive grave marker.

As promised, the graveside service lasted only five minutes. Then everyone piled back into our respective cars and headed to Oak Ridge to Nina's house. Frank told Nina he would ride with me, to keep me company. What he really wanted was to question me about what I found out at the church. He knew he wouldn't have a chance when we got to Nina's.

I tried to remember word for word what the two men had said to me.

"So Cap was essentially blackmailing Morgan, was he? That surely gives him a motive. Good work, Tommi."

"Ummm, I'm not so sure. But it's something to think about."

"And you got the info on this guy who says Cap stole his script?"

"Well, I'm going to get it from the lawyer. What a creep, though."

"I could make a statement about lawyers—thinking of Bernard here—but I won't be so crude. What did this poor dude do to piss you off?"

"He's just one of those slimy guys who thinks he's God's gift to women. I'll tell you—he's definitely not!"

When we arrived at Nina's, the house was filled with the aroma of baked ham and freshly baked bread. There were also hot casseroles, salads and desserts that friends or neighbors had dropped off on their way to the funeral. So maybe Cap's so-called popularity had been superficial, but Nina must have endeared herself to some people. While she was gone, she had hired a woman to housesit who had arranged the dishes on the long counter that separated kitchen from breakfast area. Nina and Frank and Claudia busied themselves making coffee and setting out plates and silverware while Michelle and Bill went out to the patio. I followed Daniel, Cap's brother, to the family room. It was the first opportunity I'd had to speak to him. He was a slightly stocky man in his forties who wore his thinning but wavy hair longer than was fashionable now for older men. His bushy eyebrows accentuated the hair loss even more as they bristled above dark, brooding eyes. His prominent chin jutted forth in a determined-looking face. Daniel sat down wearily in one of the chairs, his body sinking gratefully into its soft cushions. He looked haggard.

I sat down on a sofa across from him. "I haven't had a chance yet to express my condolences to you. It must be very hard to lose a brother."

He nodded sadly. "Yes, we were close."

"I understand you live in New York. Did you see much of each other? Didn't he go there on business quite often?"

"Yeah, he did. Usually like once or twice a month or so. Until this past year we got together every time." He shook his head. "Hard to believe I'll never see him again."

I wasn't sure this was an appropriate time to bring up the next question, but I didn't know if I'd ever have a chance to talk with Daniel again. I just hoped he wouldn't take offense. "Do you have any idea then who this Allison could be that Cap supposedly was having an affair with? I've heard she might be in New York."

Daniel looked surprised. "You know about her? I thought maybe Nina kinda kept it quiet. I mean it's bound to be hard on the ego when your hubby gets seriously involved with someone else. But the answer is no, I have no idea who she is. I've suspected for a long time he was having affairs. He met lots of beautiful women in his line of work. But up till recently nothing serious. Then suddenly about a year and a half ago, he started calling with excuses why he couldn't see me."

"Why was that?"

"At first I thought he was ticked off at me, but I couldn't figure out why. But when Nina finally told me about Allison, I put two-and-two together and figured he was spending all his time with her. So I suppose she does live in the city. Makes sense."

"Daniel, do you have any idea at all how we could find out who this Allison is?"

He shrugged. "I don't see how. That was one closely guarded secret he took with him into the lake. Why do you want to know anyway? What difference does it make now?"

"Maybe she had a husband or lover who wanted Cap dead. That's one of the most sensible explanations I can come up with for what happened."

Daniel appeared to ponder that thought for a while. "Well, yeah, that could be a possibility. At least it's got to be someone other than Nina. She couldn't do a thing like that."

"That seems to be the consensus with everyone but the police. This brings up a point I'd like to ask you. Nina told me once that you and Cap had periods when you barely spoke to each other."

Daniel, who had been slumped back in the chair, sat up straight. "That's not true. We got along damn well considering."

"Considering what?"

"That he could be pretty obnoxious when he was drunk. That he screwed around which I didn't approve of. But we tried not to judge each other. I had my own sins to account for. And we could have a helluva good time together."

"Why do you suppose Nina said that if it wasn't true?" I asked. Surely she wouldn't make something like that up.

"My guess is he had to come up with some excuse why he wasn't seeing me when he was in town. If she asked about me, he could just say we weren't speaking when in truth he was with Allison. He'd say anything that suited his purpose."

"Come on in and help yourselves," Nina called from the kitchen door. "There's enough food here for an army."

"Thanks for being so honest with me," I told Daniel as we got up to go to the kitchen.

"Wish I could be more help." He shrugged to indicate he really knew nothing.

Everyone filled a plate and gathered round the large breakfast table. As with most family gatherings after funerals, the talk dwelt on surface things like the weather or the latest sport scores, as if to stave off the reality of death. There was a false joviality that belied the fact of Cap's demise, and more importantly, Nina's supposed involvement. Apparently lost in her own thoughts, she sat silently picking at food as the small talk swirled around her,. I was at the opposite end of the table, and I wanted to scream at everyone to just shut up. But of course I didn't. It probably wouldn't have helped her anyway. The constant buzz of conversation gave her the chance to retreat into herself and not have to play hostess with an insincere smile on her face.

I stayed on for a while, helping to clear the table and put the dishes in the dishwasher, unsure whether Nina would prefer to be alone or felt more secure surrounded by family. Anyway, Frank and Daniel would be staying with her, Frank for an undetermined length of time, and Daniel for two or three days. He was a manufacturer's rep and had decided as long as he was in the area to call on a few local companies to see if he could pick up some new business. Michelle was going to take her brother and sister to the Greensboro airport shortly.

I questioned both Bill and Claudia when I had an opportunity to do so out of Nina's earshot. Neither of them could give me any helpful information, either on Allison or who might have wanted to harm Cap. They, like Michelle, had not had much contact with Nina and Cap for many years, except for occasional exchange of letters and very infrequent trips home. Nina had never mastered the computer and didn't even exchange e-mails with her family. Or that's what she had told me. It may have been an excuse because she simply wasn't interested in remaining in close touch with her siblings.

Michelle, Bill, and Claudia left around six-thirty. Nina suggested to Frank and Daniel that they should swim a few laps of the pool. Neither had brought trunks but Nina found some that had belonged to Cap. "They have elasticized waists," she said. "They should fit almost anyone short of King Kong. It's so hot out tonight. That will cool you off."

She and I sat alone in the family room, watching the men through the French doors.

Nina rubbed the sides of her face. She looked exhausted. "I'm so glad this day is over. I really wondered if I could make it through it."

"I know it's been tough." That was quite an understatement after all she'd been through.

"I've been thinking all day...what if? What if I'd thrown in the sponge when he told me about Allison and told him to get lost? I wouldn't be in this position now."

"Why *did* you decide to fight for him? What made you refuse to give up?" I couldn't help but think of my own life; had I given in to Bernard too easily? Would it have been possible to win him back? Would I have wanted to?

Nina ran her finger along the cording on the arm of the chair as she considered the question. "Have you ever heard of being addicted to a person?"

"Addicted?" I sounded like a parrot mimicking her, but it seemed like such a strange concept.

"Like being hooked on drugs or cigarettes or anything that's bad for you. Even though our life could be pure hell, I couldn't give him up. I don't know why, but I was sure I couldn't live without him." She looked me in the eye now. "Isn't that ironic? Now that he's gone, staying alive and getting out of this mess are all I think about."

"Did he beat you?" In all our time together, Nina always skirted the intimate details of her marriage. I don't mean their sex life, but the give and take of their everyday relationship, how he treated her. Everyone else suggested that he was a real jerk to live with, but she had never said that to me until now. She wasn't a whiner, and after that first discussion we had about Cap's infidelity the first time I visited her here, she said little about her life with Cap.

"He didn't physically abuse me. But he could get pretty nasty when he was drunk. Psychological abuse. And we'd get into screaming matches. I always swore

I'd stay calm, but I never could. But usually we'd make up soon afterward. Until Allison came along, that is. But lately it seemed that things had started to turn around. I was beginning to think my efforts were paying off and that Cap was going to stay with me. He'd actually treated me better than he had in years when he got back from California, just before he was killed. It's so sad that the argument over driving was the last time we talked to each other."

"The fact that he apparently was giving Allison up should give you some comfort. But I know there's very little right now that will be any real consolation." I felt that my words sounded stilted and rehearsed, but I was sincere. It's so hard to know how to say the right thing. "I just want you to know I'm here for you whenever you need me. Please give me a call at any time, if you need to get something off your chest or whatever. I'm a good listener."

"I wish there was something you could do to get the police off my back. Got a magic wand?" Nina gave me a lackluster smile.

I got up and hugged her. "Don't I wish!" It was almost eight-thirty when I got home. Tee met me at the door looking as starved as a twenty-pound fur-covered lump possibly could. I filled his dish with odoriferous "Ocean Bouquet," holding my breath while I spooned it out so it wouldn't turn my stomach. But he tore into it as if I'd neglected to feed him for a week. I wondered how he could get so hungry when he slept twenty-two hours a day.

Chapter *twelve*

The light on my answering machine was blinking, and when I listened to the tape, I recognized the insinuating voice immediately. Even if he hadn't given his name, the intimation of sexual innuendo was unmistakable.

"Ernie Zaleski here. You must be in the shower washing your hair. What an interesting thought." I gave silent thanks I'd turned down his offer to come over. "Anyhoo, I couldn't find Truesdale's address. Must have taken it out of my briefcase. But I remembered the aunt's name and looked it up in the local telephone book. She could tell you how to reach him. She's Evelyn Truesdale and her number is 368-9045. And, Tommi, I'm going to be in town another couple of days. Have to go over some paperwork with Nina. When you're free, why don't you give me a call at the Marriott? I'm in room 612. I gotta tell you redheads have always been my favorite."

Fat chance! If this was typical of the way people in L.A. presented themselves, no wonder Nina wanted to come back to North Carolina. That kind of tacky attempt at seduction was more the exception than the rule here.

As soon as the message finished, I dialed the number he'd given me for Truesdale's aunt..

A woman answered the phone, her voice soft and sweet.

"Is this Evelyn Truesdale?" I asked.

"Yes it is. And who might this be?"

"Tommi Poag. I'm calling about your nephew, Robert Truesdale."

"Oh, what about Robert?" She sounded concerned.

"Is it Miss or Mrs. Truesdale?"

"It's Miss." That meant she must be the sister of Robert's father, a maiden aunt.

"Well, Miss Truesdale, I wanted to get in touch with him to talk about his script. You know, the one he claims was the basis for *Astral Express*."

"Why do you want to know about that?" I could tell I had pushed her buttons.

"I'm a close friend of Nina Sellars. You know, of course, that she has been charged with her husband's death."

"Oh, yes," she said, her voice very serious now. "I heard that on the news. I never imagined that anyone I knew would ever come to that. What is this world coming to?"

Did she think Nina was guilty? There was no protestation that it couldn't be possible. It was alarming that someone who knew her could even conceive that she was capable of murder.

"What did you say your name was?" Evelyn continued.

"Poag. Tommi Poag."

"Poag! Of course. You must be related to her in some way," she exclaimed.

"In a roundabout way. She's first-cousin-once-removed to my former husband, Bernard Poag, who's also her attorney."

"Hmm. Once removed. That business always has confused me."

"Her dad and my ex are first cousins."

"Oh, yes, right." She still sounded dubious, and I didn't blame her.

"Actually, I'd like to talk to you as well as to Robert. I understand he gave the script to you to pass along to Cap."

"I used to babysit Frank Poag's kids years ago. I knew Nina when she was little, and we'd continued to trade Christmas cards over the years."

Time for some creative fibbing. I was feeling bolder about that now. "Nina had told me recently that she thought Cap had taken advantage of Robert." Actually this part was true. She had mentioned once to me that she thought Cap had used someone else's material, but she felt powerless to do anything about it. She had mentioned no names. "It bothered her a lot, especially since you were a friend of hers. She'd been thinking about compensating him some way without Cap knowing about it."

"Really?" Evelyn said. "That restores my faith in humanity."

"Of course, now with this business of Cap's death, she's got other things on her mind." What an understatement that was! I hurried on." But I want to help her out some way or other during this difficult time. I thought perhaps if I could talk with you and Robert about it and could work out a tentative agreement for her approval, it would give her the satisfaction of knowing she'd done a good deed. That would be a pleasant distraction from what she's going through." I prayed it wouldn't occur to Evelyn that Nina was surely not in a position to pay anybody anything right now. I hoped the chance to help her nephew would push any doubts from Evelyn's mind. And, frankly, she sounded somewhat naive. Shouldn't judge someone by her telephone voice, but scam artists do it every day. And I wasn't scamming her–I told myself. Just looking for information.

"You really think that in spite of what's happening to her, she'd want to do this?" So she did have some reservations.

"I'm sure of it, knowing how much it bothered her. Nina is always concerned about other people." At least that was true. Did I feel ashamed about laying it on so thick? Not really. Not if it would help uncover any bit of information that would lead me to point the finger of guilt somewhere other than straight at Nina.

"Well, sure, I'll see you," Evelyn said. "Would tomorrow morning do? I could see you about eleven. I go to early church, but would be home by then."

"That'll be fine." I didn't feel a lick of remorse knowing I'd be stretching the truth all over the place for a woman who just left a house of worship.

She gave me Robert's address and phone number in Kernersville and the number at the motel where he worked as a desk clerk.

Since he worked the evening shift, I called the Kings Inn in Kernersville where he worked on the desk, concocting a story to confirm whether or not he was working the night of Cap's death. I'm not always good at spontaneous fibbing, so I'd worked out my tale in advance in case I needed it.

"I stayed at your motel the night of September 19th," I told him. "I got talking to your desk clerk and found out he was quite a gourmet cook. We started comparing favorite recipes, and I had one he was real interested in. I promised to send it to him when I got home, but unfortunately I seem to have lost his name and address. Could you be so kind as to help me out?" I'd put on my best down-home accent to be more credible. If he only knew how I hated to cook.

"Sure. What night did you say you were here?"

"Last Wednesday, the 19th."

"Let me look it up."

There were a few minutes of silence as he checked the records.

"Okay, the night clerk on the 19th was Mack Arnold." And he gave me his address. I was surprised he'd give it out so willingly in this day and age, but I guess he thought a good old Southern belle must be harmless.

"I don't know; that name doesn't sound right," I said. "What were his hours? I want to make sure it's the right person."

"He worked from four in the afternoon till about two that night since his relief's car broke down."

"That's gotta be him then. Thanks so much for your help." I was all graciousness.

"Any time. We hope you enjoyed your stay with us."

"Oh, very much. I'll have to recommend the motel the next chance I have. You certainly have bent over backward to be accommodating." If I laid it on any thicker, I'd have to get my blood sugar checked.

So Robert Truesdale was not working that evening. I called the home number Evelyn had given me and got his answering machine. "Sorry, I'm not here. Leave a message." I wondered how the world ever managed without answering machines. I wasn't sure whether they were a blessing or a curse. Deciding it best to reach him in person, I hung up without leaving a message.

There was nothing more I could do tonight. I watched a little TV and Headline News before going to bed. Nina hadn't made it to the national news. Evidently a screenwriter didn't have the "star quality" that others in the industry had. Thank God. It was bad enough to be badgered by the local media.

Chapter
thirteen

I had planned to sleep late the next morning, but it was impossible. I woke up at 6:30, my normal weekday getting-up time, and that was that. There was too much on my mind, and it wouldn't go away. Finally, in desperation, I got up, put on my ten-year-old jogging suit, barely worn, and went for a walk around the neighborhood, the closest I ever came to exercise outside of yoga.

It was a pleasant if ordinary neighborhood, much more like the one where I grew up than the country club area where I'd lived with Bernard. Cottage Place was mostly lined with townhouses like mine with a few single family homes on one end and apartments on the other.

By 10:30 I'd returned home, showered, had a quick breakfast, and tried to reach Robby again without success. Then I left for Evelyn Truesdale's house.

Evelyn, too, lived in an older neighborhood, Guilford Hills, the kind that developers built for middle-class families in the 1950's. The houses, mostly one-story frame with three bedrooms and one bath, had gone through the cycle of falling out of fashion and then becoming popular again as younger families looked for reasonably-priced neighborhoods close to work. Unfortunately, when these neighborhoods rose in popularity, so did the prices. I guessed that Evelyn had lived in her house most of her adult life. It had the look of genteel shabbiness that often comes when a single woman, growing older, cannot quite keep up with the demands of maintaining home and yard. That is exactly why I had gone into a condominium. If we hadn't had a landscaping service when Bernard and I lived together, my brown thumb would have been the death of all plants.

As soon as I stepped out of my car, three cats, one tabby, one white, and one white with black spots, came over to check me out. I liked Evelyn already, before even meeting her.

Tufts of grass flourished in the driveway cracks, and parts of the uneven sidewalk to the front door had sunk an inch or two. Overgrown bushes covered the lower half of the windows with long tendrils reaching up toward the roof line. The open front door allowed whatever breezes there might be into the living room. Though most of these older houses had been air conditioned by now, Evelyn's seemed to be the exception.

I rang the doorbell while all three cats vied for rubbing space on my legs. I leaned down and petted them, setting up a veritable orchestration of purring. In a couple of minutes, a short roly-poly woman apparently in her sixties appeared at the door. She was dressed in a bright purple dress with matching purple shoes that gave her the appearance of a large grape. Her dark hair was skinned back tightly into a knot at the base of her neck adding to the effect. I hoped that the grin I couldn't stifle would be taken as a friendly greeting rather than my real amusement at the spectacle of Miss Truesdale, the human grape.

"You must be Mrs. Poag," Evelyn greeted me, opening the screen door and gesturing me inside. The living room was another surprise. I would have expected a clutter of traditional furniture and tables loaded with knickknacks. But instead the room was sparsely furnished with Shaker furniture, simple lines and woven seats, a far more ascetic style than one would ever expect. She may have been flamboyant in her clothing, but her house was the epitome of understatement.

She settled onto a settee and I sat in a rocking chair that was beautifully designed made from a pale wood. Evelyn removed her purple shoes and rubbed her feet vigorously.

"Sorry," she said, "but those shoes just kill me. I bought them especially to go with this dress so I feel compelled to wear them, even when I'm in agony." She made a wry face.

"I don't believe I saw you at the funeral service," I said, certain I could not have forgotten Evelyn Truesdale. Even if she'd dressed in black.

"I intended to go, but couldn't make it. You see, I'm an emergency room nurse at Wesley Long Hospital. Yesterday I worked the six-to-two shift, and I'd planned to take off a little early to get there in time. But there was a multi-car accident over on Wendover, and they started bringing in the injured, and we were overwhelmed. I didn't get out of there till after five o'clock. But the living have to take precedence over the dead, don't you know." She finally quit rubbing her feet and smoothed down the skirt of her dress.

I'd read about that in the morning paper. Seven people were hurt, most of them seriously. Some damn fool was drunk, of course.

"Isn't that the hospital where they took Cap after their accident?" I asked. We only had two in town with emergency rooms, and Wesley Long was closer to Lake Brandt.

"Yes, in fact I was there at the time. But I'm not sure what you mean by accident." She looked at me questioningly like she wondered where I was going with this line of thought.

"Well, I really don't know what to call it," I answered, "but I'm certain that Nina wasn't responsible."

"You don't agree with the police then."

"Not at all." I said it emphatically, wanting her to know where I stood on that issue. Her attitude was perplexing.

Evelyn sat up straighter, her short legs barely touching the floor. She intertwined her fingers on her lap and stared at them instead of looking at me.

"Well, I don't know," she said. "Of course it's very hard for me to believe that Nina had anything to do with it. But the whole affair is very strange. I don't know what to think."

"What do you mean?"

"I mean the way Cap died."

I didn't think that the media had the information yet that Nina was supposed to have pushed the car into the water. Could Evelyn know about it somehow? "His drowning?"

"He didn't die from drowning."

I couldn't believe my ears. "What do you mean? Nina said they temporarily revived him, but he died in the emergency room. Isn't that considered dying from drowning?"

"Not when the doctors felt he had a good chance at recovery, even though he might have sustained some brain damage." Evelyn was shaking her head at the tragedy of it.

"Are you trying to say you don't think he died of natural causes? That someone deliberately caused his death in the hospital?"

"He was stable enough to leave alone. The nurses and doctors were in and out, but it was a very busy night, and no one could stay with him every minute. Besides it didn't seem necessary. We were waiting for a room to open up so we could transfer him. Then, an hour after they brought him in, he suddenly was dead. No medical personnel were in the room at the time."

"Was Nina with him?"

"Yes. That was one reason we felt he'd be okay. She could notify us if there was any difficulty."

"Did she ever leave him alone, even for a minute?"

"I can't say for sure. I was too busy to keep track. She might have gone to the restroom or to make phone calls."

"Did they do an autopsy?"

"Oh yes. But the results aren't back as far as I know. That takes a while."

My God. One more hurdle to get over. We could surely do without another surprise. I wondered why Nina hadn't told me this. Had she been aware that the doctors felt that he would survive the near drowning? Did she realize that suspicion surrounded the time she spent at the hospital? This revelation left me totally unnerved, but I didn't want Evelyn to be aware of it. so I regrouped.

"Changing the subject, I wasn't able to reach Robert last night or this morning, but I'll keep trying," I said. "You don't happen to know where he is, do you?"

"No, it's not like he has to check in with Auntie all the time. We have a standing date on the last Sunday of the month when we have lunch and get caught up on each other. I don't want him to think I'm hovering over him."

"Could you tell me a little bit about him?" Since Evelyn had no children of her own, it was probable that Robert would be very close to her, the way nieces and nephews often are to childless women. I had a special place in my heart for my own niece and nephew. Unfortunately they lived a thousand miles away.

"Oh, yes. Robby's such a talented boy." Evelyn was gushing now. "Well," she giggled, "he's no longer a boy, of course; he's twenty-seven. But he's wanted to be a writer since he was knee high to a grasshopper, always writing little stories for his teachers when he was in school. He even took that night job so he would have time to write."

I could tell I'd hit on a favorite subject and felt confident enough to go on. "Why did he give you the script instead of sending it directly to Cap?"

"He'd tried and tried to break into the movie business, but all he ever got was rejections. He knew that I used to babysit Nina and that her husband was a big shot writer in Hollywood. So out of frustration, he asked if I'd send them a script and put in a good word for him. He'd tried everything else to sell one, and it never worked. He figured having any kind of a connection was better than none at all. And he'd always admired Cap's work and hoped they could work on it together."

"And how long ago was this?"

"Mmmm. Let me think" Evelyn twirled a citrine ring around on her pudgy finger. "Three or four years ago. I can't remember exactly for sure."

Long enough that it could have been the basis for the movie script.

"Did you by any chance read it?" I asked.

"Yes I did. I take great interest in his work."

"And have you seen the movie *Astral Express*?"

"I sure did. And it was so much like Robby's script. I was shocked because I knew Robby hadn't received any money or credit for it."

"How did he feel about that?" Kind of a silly question considering. But I wanted to know the depth of his anger.

"Pretty upset, naturally. He wanted credit. And the money. On the other hand he was elated that they liked his idea enough to use it. If Nina were to do something for him, I know it would at least help to make up for the hurt he suffered."

"Well, I'll do my best to see what we can work out. And I thank you for your time."

"Just help my darling boy get what he deserves."

Driving home, I thought about Evelyn's last remark. I hoped I could do that. If it turned out that he was responsible for Cap's death, there's nothing I would rather do than get him what he deserved: a nice long term in jail. On the other hand, if he was an innocent victim of Cap's greed and duplicity, I thought I could convince Nina to help him out, once all this mess was straightened out. God willing that it *got* straightened out.

Chapter
fourteen

After a quick lunch of salad and drink at Wendy's, I went to the main library next where I spent a couple of hours checking over the society columns in the *Greensboro News and Record*. I began with the previous spring, the last time Cap had been in town, and worked backward to the time the Sellars moved to Oak Ridge. As Michelle had told me, Nina and Cap's names appeared frequently as guests at parties and fund raisers sponsored by the country club set. I made a list of couples' names who appeared most often at the same events, making a check mark for each time they were mentioned. I ended up with a list of five couples who seemed to have been at most of the functions together with the Sellars. The names were all familiar, a "Who's Who" of the socially elite of Greensboro. I'd met some of them from time to time, but even as the wife of Bernard Poag, a highly successful attorney, I had not belonged in the same stratum as these folks. I then looked up each couple in the city directory for addresses and phone numbers. Surprisingly they were all listed. I wasn't sure I'd speak to all of them, but I wanted to meet at least a couple of the women. They, rather than their husbands, might be able to give me some insight into the Sellars' relationship. Women are a lot more intuitive about marriages than men are. Thus armed, I returned home.

About nine-thirty that evening Frank called.

"Hi, I wanted to talk to you when Nina wasn't around. She and Daniel just went off to a drugstore."

"How's it going?"

"Being here puts me somewhat at a disadvantage. It's hard to find a time when I can call people or check into things since I don't want them to know what I'm doing. Find out anything new?"

I told him about my attempt to reach Robert Truesdale and described my visit with his aunt.

"Hey, when you say you'll give it a shot, you mean it in spades, don't you? What do you think we should do now?"

"I'm going to keep trying to reach Robert. I called a few minutes ago but still got his answering machine. As for Morgan, he told me he was in L.A. when Cap died. I'm not sure how to check that out, though Ernie Zaleski might be able to help. But to tell you the truth, I really can't stand that man. Why don't you talk to him? See what he was doing that night too because he didn't say. You can reach him at the O.Henry Hotel."

"I'll do it right now while Nina's still gone. You've done everything so far, so I'd like to get some licks in too. Anything else?"

"Can't think of anything. Oh, except I'm going to try to contact some of Cap's high society friends."

"What do you think they can tell you? Other than how much he drank, and how he chased the women."

"Well, who knows? He might have confided in someone who his Lady Love was, though I doubt it. I just felt that some of the women, particularly, could tell me how Cap and Nina were when they were together. I've heard a lot about their quarrel the night he died, but I'd like to know how they normally acted toward one another. Not ever having met Cap, it's hard for me to get a fix on him."

"Good idea. Since I was his father-in-law, he no doubt tried to put his best foot forward when we were together. So I probably don't have a true picture of him either. Even then I didn't like him much. I could tell Nina was holding things back from me."

"I'm sure the cops haven't analyzed Cap the way I'm trying to do. But, let's face it, I don't have a whole heck of a lot to go on otherwise. If Cap was making enemies, the more I know, no matter how much it seems unrelated, the more it will help me. At least I hope so."

"Well, since it's so late, I'll wait till tomorrow to report back to you on my conversation with Zaleski. Talk to you then."

I read a little then went to bed and fell into a deep sleep. I dreamed about a demolition derby where every car was driven by someone I'd seen in the past couple of days: Bernard, Nina, Frank, Michelle, Ernie Zaleski, Daniel, Morgan Proxmire. They were crashing into one another with great relish in an attempt to eliminate each other from the competition. But it seemed as if all the cars were incapacitated simultaneously, and all the drivers sat in their smashed up, inoperable cars, glowering at each other. It had become a standoff, a deadlock. I was the referee (did such events have referees I wondered in my sleep?) and I was helpless. No one could move; no one would get out of his or her car.

Something wet and warm was rubbing my face. It was as if I was being pulled back from another world when I woke up during a dream. Reluctantly I opened my eyes, focusing them on the digital clock on the night stand. It said 11:49. Then I tried to figure out what had awakened me. Tee was next to my head, mewing in his soft, insistent voice. He always slept at the foot of my bed, and regularly at 6:30 a. m. he would summon me to feed him by pulling at the bedclothes with his front paws and crying pitifully. Now he was pawing my pillow, and evidently he'd been licking my face. This was not like him. Had I forgotten to feed him? No, I distinctly remembered filling his bowl.

I half sat up, annoyed that he would wake me at such a god-awful hour. I hated not knowing how my dream was going to end. Realizing reluctantly I'd have to give him more food or he'd keep this up, I swung my feet over the edge of the bed and started to reach for my robe in the nearby chair. My eyes had finally grown accustomed to the dark, and I noticed a strange mistiness in the air. Oh, God! My heart began to race; dread made my legs unsteady and caused bile to rise in my throat. I went to the door, and the mistiness turned into smoke in the hallway, swirling near the ceiling and around the silent smoke alarm.

At the bottom of the stairs I could see a red glow from downstairs filtered through dense smoke as though through a coated lens. I knew I'd never get through that. I'd have to go out the bedroom window.

Shaking with fright, I tried to think straight. What should I do? Keep the fire out of my room first seemed obvious. I slammed the door shut, wet a bath towel in the adjoining bathroom, and jammed it against the crack at the door's bottom. The window over the patio–that would be the best way out. Prickly pyracantha bushes under the side window would tear up my skin if I went out that way. I shoved out the screen of the window on the rear wall and looked down. The patio table with the umbrella was about a dozen feet away. I could throw Tee onto its canvas top so he could jump to the ground from there. Picking him up from the bed, I hugged him for a minute. "I know you can do it, Tee. Do it for me." Then I leaned out the window, extending my arms as far as I could considering he felt like a ton of rocks, and tossed him toward the umbrella. He plummeted like a lead weight, his legs splayed, and hit it not far from the edge. He tried to hold on, but his claws slid on the slick yellow canvas, and he plunged off the edge and landed on the cement patio. For a minute he was still. The landing seemed to have shocked him into momentary insensibility, but at last he stood up, shook himself, and walked slowly toward the open gate in the fence.

Throwing the blanket aside, I tugged the top sheet from my bed. I tried ripping it without success, so I searched frantically through the medicine cabinet for my manicure scissors. Even though my hands shook badly, and the scissors were too small, I finally snipped through the edge and ripped the sheet into strips. With silent thanks to my Girl Scout training, I tied the strips together with square knots, then tied one end to a bedpost of the four poster that had been my grandmother's. The post appeared pretty fragile; I wasn't at all sure it would hold my weight. Right now I wished I could take long leaps to safety like Tee, to say nothing of having nine lives.

Modesty won out even over terror, and I threw on my robe over my very brief and sheer nightie. Swinging one leg over the windowsill, I craved athletic ability more than I ever had in my life. The sheet-rope hung down to the patio where it ended about two feet above the ground. I hated heights, and the ground seemed so far away it made me dizzy. But I had no choice.

Grasping the rope tightly, I maneuvered my other leg through the open window, then ducking down, I squirmed through as I twisted my body to face the wall. My terror made my body stiff, and I held myself away from the rough surface of the brick wall with my tender bare feet. I was suspended above the utility room window with nowhere to go but down.

As I hung there, I heard the sound of glass breaking and saw flames as the fire roared through the window beneath me. I could no longer go straight down. The flames, although they did not yet reach me, gave off almost unbearable heat. So I planted my feet firmly against the wall, my knees bent, and catapulted myself as far out into the air as I could, letting go of the sheet rope at the furthest point, dropping six or seven feet onto the patio, just missing the table and umbrella. I remembered to flex my knees when I hit the ground and put out my hands to catch myself. I felt a stab of pain in my left wrist as I landed and fell back in a sprawl on the concrete, scraping my elbow.

I lay there stunned, wondering how much damage I'd done to my body. When I looked up, I saw the end of the sheet rope catch fire as it dangled in front of the window, and like a wick, burn rapidly upward toward the bedroom.

Chapter fifteen

Garnet Langdon, my next-door neighbor, came tearing through the gate in the privacy fence. She bent over me trying to determine how badly I was hurt. She looked as frightened as I felt.

"Tommi, are you okay?" She hovered over me, but was reluctant to touch me for fear of inflicting more damage.

"As far as I can tell," I said, rubbing my sore arm. "I think my wrist is sprained; at least it doesn't seem to be broken. Otherwise, I think everything is working all right."

Relief flooded her face. "I was watching the late news, and Sheppie needed to go out. When I let her out the back door, I could see this strange glow over here, so I came around to the gate to investigate and saw the fire. I went around and pounded on your front door, but you must not have heard me. And of course it was locked. I was so afraid you'd been overcome by smoke. The only thing I could do was run home and call the fire department."

"Tee woke me or I'd probably be dead from smoke inhalation. For some reason my smoke alarm didn't go off. I don't understand that because I recently put in a new battery."

"Let me help you out of here, then I'll go out front and flag down the firemen." Garnet bent over to grasp me under the arms.

"No, no, I don't want to leave; I want to stay," I protested. "How about getting one of those chairs for me." I gestured toward the metal chairs around the table. The flames from the window were licking the edge of the umbrella now, but I hoped the chair on the far side of the table wouldn't be too hot to touch. "Be careful," I warned, "don't burn yourself."

Garnet flicked her hand across the top of the chair checking its temperature and then picked it up and carried it to the far corner of the patio, as much out of harm's way as possible. She grabbed me under the arms and helped me to my feet and steadied me as I walked slowly to the chair.

"Let me go flag down the firemen," she said and ran out the gate and around to the front to await them. I could now hear the distant wail of the fire truck. The piercing sounds grew rapidly louder, and soon I could tell they were on my street. The cacophony stopped abruptly, leaving a momentary silence that was soon filled with men shouting orders and the sound of the pumper.

Three firemen dressed in turnout gear and wearing breathing masks ran onto the patio, two of them carrying a smallish hose. I was surprised at how small it was. In the movies they always seemed to be wielding hoses like mammoth writhing snakes. The third fireman checked the sliding glass door. When he saw that a metal rod in the track held it shut, he broke the glass with a tool he was carrying, dislodged the rod and opened the door.

Two more firemen entered the patio and rushed into the house with the one who opened the door, past the burning laundry room into the hall and up the stairs.

Garnet came over to me and put her hand on my shoulder. "You okay?" she asked.

I wasn't, but I smiled bravely up at my neighbor and nodded yes. "Didn't you tell them nobody was in there?"

"I did, but they said they wanted to check it out anyway."

The two firemen with the hose had followed the others through the sliding door and stood at the laundry room door directing the water onto the flames that filled the room. Within thirty seconds the flames disappeared, and smoke billowed out of the door and window and drifted upward, obscuring the stars on this cloudless night.

All those flames and all that smoke. I couldn't believe it could be over so quickly. After the firemen carried the hose back across the patio and out the gate, another one with a large flashlight came over to where I was sitting. He was a homely man with an acne scarred face but with an air of quiet authority. "I'm Battalion Chief Holmes," he said. "Are you all right?"

"I think I've sprained my wrist is all. I came out the bedroom window." I pointed toward the open window where a short charred piece of bed sheet hung limply over the sill.

"Have any problems from the smoke?"

"No. I got out before much of it got in the bedroom."

"Well, I'm going in and take a look around then."

He spent forty-five minutes inside. I couldn't see him from my vantage point but assumed he was checking to make sure the fire wouldn't reignite as well as trying to determine the cause. I was torn between wanting to see the damage and not wanting to see it. How much of my home had been destroyed? What was I going to do?

Garnet tried to make small talk, but I couldn't even pretend to carry on a conversation. After a few unrewarded attempts, Garnet finally remained quiet too. She had pulled another chair away from the table and sat in silence beside me. I was grateful for her presence. I hoped she realized how much I appreciated her kindness.

Finally Chief Holmes came out of the house and walked over to me. "Your smoke alarm wasn't working. Don't you ever check it?"

"Yes, of course," I protested. "I changed the batteries recently. I don't know why it didn't work."

"We'll check the batteries out to see if they were dead or whether it malfunctioned."

"How did it start? And how bad is the damage?" I could hardly bring myself to ask the questions. It was if not knowing the worst kept it from being true.

"It looks as though you left your iron on...and face down, which got it started. Then the laundry and cleaning supplies really got it going." His voice was even and without rebuke, though his expression was stern.

I found that unthinkable. I had pressed my clothes before going to see Evelyn Truesdale, but was sure I'd turned the iron off and left it upright. Maybe my memory had occasional lapses now and then, but I couldn't believe I'd do anything that dumb. Besides, it couldn't take that many hours to ignite.

And I said so to Chief Holmes.

"Ma'am, I'm sorry, but the evidence is there. You were home alone, weren't you?"

"Yes."

"And how long had you been in the house tonight?"

"Since about five."

"You didn't use the iron this evening?"

"Not since morning."

"What about pets? Do you have any pets?"

Oh God, in the turmoil I'd forgotten about Tee. Where was poor Tee? "I have a cat." I hoped I still had one.

He smiled at me, took off his hat and wiped the sweat from his forehead with the sleeve of his coat. "The cat could have knocked it over and played with the dial. Do you usually leave it plugged in?"

I could feel my face flush. "Well, yes, I do."

"Okay," he said, "there's your answer."

I couldn't believe it, but there was no ,sense in arguing the point now. Tee would be branded the official culprit in this fire. I knew I couldn't convince him otherwise. I pushed myself upright with my right arm, leaning on the chair arm for support. "Can I get in now and see it?"

"You'll need something on your feet. There's broken glass in there," he warned me.

"My shoes are all upstairs in my closet."

"I'll send one of the men up for some," he said and went back in the house.

"What about clothes?" Garnet asked when he left.

I looked down at my soiled and torn bathrobe and shrugged. "Looks like I'll need some to go to the emergency room. My mother always told me to wear clean underwear in case I was ever in an accident. I guess you should keep extra clothes somewhere in case your house burns down too." It was a pretty lame joke, but I had to either try for a little humor or break down and cry. And I was damned if I would do that in front of her and the firefighters.

Garnet smiled for the first time. "Right. You keep an emergency pack at my house, and I'll keep one at yours. But in this case you'll have to hope your clothes don't smell too bad from the smoke. As soon as they let us in, get yourself some, and I'll take you to the hospital."

"You're a lifesaver, Garnet."

A fireman brought me a pair of canvas shoes, and we followed Chief Holmes through the broken sliding door into the house. He played the light of his lantern over the rooms to show me the damage. I had braced myself for what I would find, but surprisingly, although it was blackened with soot and the floor was running with water, the kitchen seemed pretty much intact. But the laundry room, which opened off the kitchen, was in total shambles. The cabinets were charred, the appliances blackened, the walls burnt through in spots. And an acrid smell permeated the house.

"Outside of the laundry room, most of the damage is from smoke and water," Chief Holmes told me. "Everything's under control now. Maybe you'd better go have that wrist tended to. We'll get back in touch with you later about our findings, though I'm sure your cat is the culprit. Now do you have a flashlight so you can find your things?"

"There should be one in the kitchen drawer," I said. "Let me check."

He aimed his lantern on the cabinets while I hunted for it. I hoped to heaven the batteries were not dead in it too. That would have been really embarrassing. In fact, it worked fine.

" Okay, we're leaving now. Let us know where you'll be staying," he said.

"With me," Garnet said immediately.

"Thanks, but no," I said, grateful for her help but unwilling to impose any further. "I'll check into a motel."

As soon as the fire engines pulled away, I went upstairs and found my running suit, figuring the give of the knitted fabric would be easy to get on over my sore wrist. The upstairs smelled terrible, and everything was covered with soot, but otherwise was unharmed.

Garnet drove me to the hospital where I had an interminable wait until they could examine my wrist and X-ray it. Who knew so many people would need emergency treatment in the middle of the night. But they finally got around to me, the least critical of all the cases. I was right; it was only a sprain. But it was still darn sore. They wrapped it up and advised me to use it as little as possible while it healed.

It was now after four a.m., and Garnet again insisted that I come home with her.

"You're sweet and I appreciate it, but really, I think a motel is where I need to be. Lord knows how long it will be before I can move back in my house. If you'll take me home, I'm sure I can drive myself. With the power steering I can manage fine with one good hand."

We said good night in front of my house. From the street, everything appeared normal. I went around the side to the patio, hoping against hope that Tee would be there. But he was not. A street light shining through the kitchen window lit up the charred laundry room enough to see the destruction. I'd felt numb the past several hours, but now reality was washing over me like waves of ice water, brutally forcing me to take stock of my situation. I sat in the chair in the corner of the patio and finally cried, mostly for Tee, but also at the state my house was in. It was going to be a while before things were anywhere near back to normal.

Chapter
sixteen

I packed as much clothing as my one suitcase would hold. As I left, I decided to leave the gate to the patio open in case Tee came back, even though it allowed my shattered sliding door to be visible from the common area. I'd call someone first thing in the morning to board it and the laundry window up and pray in the meantime no one burglarized my house.

I drove to Mi Casa a few streets away, a faux-Spanish-style motel that dated to the fifties. It had always struck me as quaint, sandwiched between a Greek Revival bank and a Victorian-era home that now housed a beauty salon. Red tile roofs and stuccoed walls were a rarity in this area. But it had the reputation of being clean and affordable if far from luxurious. The small office was dimly lit by a night light, and the door was locked. But I found a doorbell to summon help and pushed it three times. After several minutes a sleepy, somewhat disheveled man shuffled out from a back room and opened the door for me. He motioned me into the office.

"Kinda late, missy," he said, not unkindly, as he tied a second knot in his bathrobe belt and smoothed down the few long hairs that were meant to hide his shiny bald head. He had the appearance of unraveling with his hair sticking out wildly in all directions.

"Sorry to get you up, but I had a fire in my house. I need a place to stay," I replied.

"Fire! Oh, my heavens!" he exclaimed, patting my arm in sympathy. "That's just terrible. And it looks like you hurt your wrist. What happened?"

I told him as briefly as possible, wanting to end this conversation and get to bed.

"Your cat, huh? I have two of them. Oh, yes, they can be mischief makers all right. I remember one time when..." His hands fluttered as he talked, gesturing dramatically.

"Sir...," I interrupted, knowing I would collapse with fatigue if I had to stand there one more minute.

"Oh, please, do call me Roger," he insisted.

"Roger, if you don't mind, I'd like to get registered so I can get to bed. And it looks like I might be staying quite a while. Until they get my place fixed."

"Of course, of course. How could I be so insensitive. You must be totally exhausted." He pulled out the registration book from under the counter and had me sign in. "Here's your key. Room twelve. And you be sure to let me know if you need anything, hon. Such a shame."

I drove the short distance to the room, unlocked the door and flicked on the light switch. The room was paneled in knotty pine and had worn reddish brown carpeting reminiscent of the red dirt outside. The dark green curtains only added to the gloominess, but I decided to pretend I was camping out in a woodsy clearing as I had years ago as a Girl Scout.

Twin beds flanked the beige laminated wall-hung night stand that matched the dresser on the opposite wall. I was horrified when I caught a glimpse in the mirror of my fatigue-drawn face and the wild mass of red curls erupting from my head at odd angles. In all the confusion I'd forgotten to comb my hair. Roger and I would make quite a pair, I thought. Exhibit A at the hairdressers' convention.

I set my suitcase on the faded orange chenille spread of the nearest bed, marveling that all these furnishings had survived this long. They had to be original; it would be impossible to buy such ugly things unless you found them in a second-hand shop. Although the furniture had a well-worn look, it had been kept in good repair, and the room was clean and fairly spacious as motel rooms go. Thank God there was a large closet for my clothes, and the bathroom had a bathtub where I could take my relaxing "soaks." But best of all there was a small refrigerator in the corner of the room. I decided it wouldn't be too great an ordeal to spend some time in this room.

I stripped to my underwear and crawled gratefully into bed. But in spite of my exhaustion, sleep would not come. My mind was filled with the terror of the evening and the events went around and around like an over-wound music box that couldn't be stopped.

The disappearance of Tee was hardest to accept. The condo could be repaired, but what if Tee never returned? I'd go back every day to look for him. Surely when he got hungry, he'd return looking for food. And hungry was his middle name.

The so-called cause of the fire troubled me greatly. The fireman was convinced that Tee had started it by knocking over the iron. But he was far less agile than most cats; his twenty pounds weighted him down, and he never jumped up on tables or counters. I doubted he could leap that high. It just didn't make sense. But what other explanation was there? It seemed ominous to me that it had happened while I was looking into Cap's death. A mere coincidence? The fact that the house was securely locked, and the fire began inside made me feel all the more vulnerable. If someone could do that, what else would he be capable of?

By seven-thirty I had slept only fitfully, waking up with a start many times as I relived those terrifying minutes when I discovered the fire and had to climb out the window. At least I was on the ground floor here. I didn't think I could ever again stay anywhere higher than two stories. I preferred ground level, but I wasn't going to sell my condo just because it had a second floor. I would buy one of those emergency rope ladders though. That would be a lot better than trying to escape down a rope made of sheets.

I felt slightly better after showering, and once I'd dressed in a flowered skirt and blue blouse, I made a list of all the people I needed to call: a carpenter to board up the broken window and door, my homeowners' insurance agent, Logan, and Nina.

Mr. Tobin, who had often done odd jobs for me, agreed to go over immediately and secure the back of my house. My insurance agent made arrangements for an adjuster to meet me at the condo at three in the afternoon to assess the damage. Logan's first reaction was to ask me if I had adequate insurance coverage.

"Well, I sure hope so," I told him. "I'll know better after I meet with the adjuster this afternoon."

His voice became quite somber then. "I hate to be the bearer of more ill tidings, but I think Nina has another huge problem."

I didn't think I could take any more bad news. "Oh, no. What now?"

"I just got a call from our home office. It seems they've determined that the signature on that recent application for additional insurance was forged. They're probably contacting the Greensboro police right this minute."

I felt like throwing up. "I can't believe it. Have you told her yet?"

"I thought it would be better if it came from you, since she's your friend." Logan was so soft hearted he always avoided having to relay unpleasant news whenever he could. It wasn't the first time he'd made me be the patsy. But this time I couldn't argue with his reasoning.

"Oh, Logan. It seems like everything is out of control. The more I try to help, the worse it gets."

"That's not *your* fault."

"I know. But I'm beginning to feel like a jinx."

"Well, you're doing everything you can. You shouldn't feel that way."

After we hung up, I reluctantly dialed Nina's number, dreading this conversation as much as anything I'd ever done. When Nina answered I told her first about the fire, though I said nothing about my suspicions concerning it. Nina became very upset, she was a mess emotionally anyway, and begged me to come stay with her till my house had been repaired.

"I need to be in Greensboro," I told her. "I'll be back to work in a few days, and I'll want to supervise the repair work too. But I appreciate the offer." I knew it would be much more difficult to do any investigating if I were staying at her house. It had tied Frank's hands to a certain extent; I didn't want mine tied too. I took a deep breath before proceeding. "It seems I have more bad news for you." I was afraid this might push Nina's fragile emotional state over the edge. "That insurance that Cap applied for? Remember that he didn't have to go through a physical or anything because he had a guaranteed purchase option on his other policy, so all he had to do was apply for it?"

"Sure, I remember."

"But he had a deadline to meet so you were going to send the application to California for him to sign."

"Oh, yes..." Nina's voice faded a little, sounded hesitant.

"Nina, our home office called Logan this morning and told him the signature had been forged."

Silence.

"Nina. Are you there? Are you okay?"

I heard a sharp intake of breath. "Oh, Tommi." The tone of her voice said everything. I knew she had done it.

"What happened, Nina? Tell me what happened." At this particular moment I wanted to wring her neck, but I tried not to let it show in my voice.

Nina's voice had a dead quality to it now. "I really screwed up this time, didn't I? Cap had called and asked me to take care of making the arrangements for the insurance and to send him the papers to sign. I'm so used to having him handle all the business things. I meant to send it, I really did, but it totally slipped my mind. All of a sudden I realized it was the last day to get it in, so I signed it myself trying to make it look like Cap's signature, and brought it to your office. I knew he'd be furious if I let the thing lapse because of my stupidity, so I guess I was thinking more about his reaction than I was about the legality of it."

"I don't know what to say to you, Nina. You might have gotten away with it under normal circumstances, but I doubt it even then. But because of Cap's death, they're scrutinizing everything. I'm sure you know how bad this looks." I tried not to be cruel, but Nina had to know what she was up against. "Even if you're found innocent, you won't be able to collect on that insurance."

"I don't *give* a damn about the money. All I was thinking about was keeping the peace with Cap." Her voice was fraught with emotion.

"I believe you. And I never hated anything as much as I hated telling you this. But I thought it'd be a little easier coming from me than learning about it from the police."

Nina didn't speak as that sank in. Finally, she tried very hard to sound brave, although I knew she was anything but. "I understand, Tommi. This will give me a chance to talk to Bernard first. Maybe he can help me put the best face on it."

Good luck I thought. There's not a whole lot you can do with that. I believed her, knowing Nina's naiveté and her desire not to upset Cap, but I doubted very much the police would.

Now it was even more urgent that I pursue what leads I had. Nina's predicament was worse than ever. I called Robert Truesdale's number again. I was surprised when a tired voice answered after the fourth ring.

"Mr. Truesdale?"

"Yes?"

"This is Tommi Poag. I've been trying to reach you since yesterday morning."

"Oh, sorry. I've been out of town on vacation since last Monday. Just got in late last night. Is it something important?" I could hear him yawn.

I rapidly shifted gears mentally. If he'd been gone, chances were good he didn't yet know about Cap's death, unless, of course, he was the one responsible. There had been nothing about it in our paper this morning, and I doubted the Kernersville paper would have carried it. I could present myself as a go-between for Nina as I did with Evelyn, but act as if Cap were still alive. Unless he was a superb actor, I believed I could tell from his demeanor whether or not he knew about Cap which could mean he was involved in his murder.

"I'm calling on behalf of Nina Sellars," I said, awaiting his reaction.

He said nothing for a moment. Was he deciding how to respond? "Oh. You mean Cap Sellars' wife?"

"Right. She got in touch with me because she felt I could be a go-between for her. She wants to do something to make up for the fact he took your script, and of course she doesn't want Cap to know she is doing this." I wished I could see Robert's face, what his expression was. "I was wondering if I might drive over and talk to you about it this morning."

"Of course!" He sounded wide awake now and almost jubilant. "She really wants to help me?"

"That's what she says. If I start out now, I could be there about ten."

"Please do come. That is great!"

Before leaving town, I drove to my condo to see if Tee had come back, but there was no sign of him. Depressed now, I had a sudden urge for a doughnut and coffee so I went to a Krispy Kreme drive-through, ordered not one but two cream-filled ones, and ate my breakfast as I headed toward the highway. I'd have to ask Roger if I could bring my microwave and coffee maker over to my room. It would be too expensive to eat all my meals out.

I drove west on I-40 toward Kernersville wondering about Robert Truesdale. Would he be the talented and aggrieved young man that his aunt claimed or a cynical manipulator trying to make a fast buck off Cap? I knew I couldn't trust Evelyn's judgment. She'd be blinded by love.

Chapter
seventeen

Robert Truesdale's apartment was in a huge old Victorian house on a street near the center of Kernersville. I could tell it had been divided into apartments some years ago because the outdoor stairs tacked onto both ends of the house needed paint as badly as the siding. When I reached the front porch, I noticed that there was rust on the six mailboxes nailed up beside the handsome front door with its oval beveled glass. The door was all that remained to recall the house's past glory. It looked as though someone had lovingly refinished it in spite of the fact that everything else had been let go for years.

I rang the bell beside Truesdale's name, and within minutes a young redheaded man came from behind the grand staircase visible through the oval glass and opened the door for me.

His glance went first to my red hair and then to my face and his smile widened, as if he'd met a long-lost relative.

"Mrs. Poag?" When I nodded, he said, "Come on in." I now understood why his Aunt Evelyn referred to him as Robby. It fit him so well. He had that all-American-boy-of-Irish-descent look, well scrubbed, light freckles, contagious smile. "My apartment is down this hall."

He led the way down a narrow hall, its floor covered in threadbare carpet and the walls in floral wallpaper that had yellowed with age, to a partially open door. He preceded me into a small living room, its single window looking out on the brick wall of the neighboring house just across a driveway. There was a flowered sofa and matching chair, a thirties' style floor lamp, and books everywhere, overflowing a five-shelf bookcase, the top of a nondescript coffee table, and even stacked on the floor. A rickety typewriter table held an electric typewriter beside the bedroom door. Evidently he couldn't even afford a computer. I could imagine his aunt in this room more easily than Robby. Perhaps she had given him her old furniture so she could buy new. Robby quite obviously had little money or else spent what he had on books.

"Please sit down, Mrs. Poag," he said. "Coffee?"

"No thanks," I replied, settling into the chair.

Robby sat on the end of the sofa nearest me. "It was nice of you to come. You say Mrs. Sellars wants to help me?"

Wanting to control the conversation as much as possible, I changed the subject. "So you've been on vacation for a week? How nice. Where'd you go?"

"The beach, Topsail. A friend has a condo there he lets me use now and then."

"How great to have a place available like that. Did you go with friends?"

"No, I always go alone. It's my chance to work on my writing undisturbed. I don't go out, not even to eat while I'm there. I even turn the phone off so I won't be interrupted. I realize that must sound pretty strange since most people go to the beach to socialize or lie around on the sand. But it's the only time I can write nonstop, and I get more done there than during the whole rest of the year. Nose to the grindstone and all that. We writers can be a strange lot, I guess. Obsessed is the word."

So there was no way to verify he'd actually been at Topsail. But he had no reason to lie to me.

"I admire your dedication. Now, why I'm here. This is just an exploratory session," I wanted to emphasize the uncertain nature of it. "I can't make any promises or commitments, but Nina wanted me to feel you out on this. She thinks that Cap used your idea in his script for *Astral Express* even though he denied it even to her. The problem is this. She feels you should have some compensation for your ideas. But she doesn't want Cap to have any bad publicity."

Robby sat looking down at the floor, drumming his fingers on the arm of the sofa, deep in thought. Finally he looked up at me. "In other words, she'd pay me off if I don't file the suit."

"I repeat, there's nothing definite. I'm just here to see what you'd say."

Robby got up and strode over to the window, though there was little to see but the brick wall. "I'd like to get credit for the idea. It would do a lot to boost my career. But as you can see, I sure could use some money. I don't know. Maybe I should just accept her offer and work like crazy on my current script. I know that if I pursue my case, it will take away from my writing time. I've already lost too much time over it."

"It must have been a real shock when you saw the movie and recognized your script," I said.

He turned to me with a wry smile. "Yeah, it was funny. I've never been so exhilarated and so angry at the same time. It gave me such a high to see my story on the screen, but I couldn't believe that he'd stolen it from me."

"How do you feel toward Cap? Silly question, I guess, but I'm curious."

Robby shrugged and sat again on the sofa. "Mixed emotions I guess. I've always admired him a lot, think his screenplays are some of the best to come out of Hollywood. When I asked Aunt Evelyn to send my script to Mrs. Sellars with a personal note, I was hoping she'd plead my case and at least get him to read it. I know guys like him must get dozens of treatments and throw them away without ever taking a look, so to have a personal connection was pure serendipity. But once it was sent off, I never heard a thing. Never knew whether they even got it. Yet, that movie was so close to my script, it was obvious he used my ideas. There was even dialogue I wrote, word for word." He hugged himself and rocked forward and back, staring at the ceiling. "I just couldn't believe he'd do such a thing." He was quiet for half a minute, deep in thought. "I think if he'd just admit to me personally that it *was* my idea, I might be satisfied. It'd be enough to know he thought my work was that good. And better yet, if he would agree to work with me on another script, I would definitely forget about *Astral Express*. With his name on the new one along with mine, it would be sure to sell."

I smiled and nodded. But I was wondering is this guy for real? Would a writer be satisfied with private recognition alone? But if Cap *had* cooperated with him writing a new script, it quite possibly could have jump-started his career and that would have been good enough. One thing I had to say about him though: he didn't *appear* to know Cap was dead.

"What do you want me to tell Nina?" I asked.

"Tell her exactly what I said. I'd prefer to have Cap confess that he stole my work and co-write a new one with me. Otherwise, I'll consider her offer."

I said I would get back to him.

He shook my good hand enthusiastically when I left. "It's sure been good to meet you, Mrs. Poag."

"Same here, Robby." I just couldn't imagine this eager young man trying to put one over on me.

But driving back to Greensboro I started to have second thoughts and decided that this visit had done little but muddy the waters. Robert Truesdale wouldn't be the first person to boldly lie with a straight face. Perhaps he was as good an actor as he was a writer. But what if he'd been telling the truth? What was he going to think of me when he learned that I was feeding him a line of bullshit? I hoped that when all was said and done, if Robby was innocent and had been wronged by Cap, that somehow he would get his due when all this mess was straightened out. But Nina's predicament took precedence over everything else.

When I arrived back at my room, the message light on my phone was blinking. I called the desk.

"Oh, yes," chirped Roger, "a Mr. Frank Poag asked that you call him."

Frank answered the phone immediately as if he had been hovering over it. "Tommi! Are you okay?" His voice was full of concern.

"I'm fine." That was definitely an exaggeration. I was still tired and my wrist hurt like hell.

"Why didn't you talk to me when you called Nina this morning?"

"Don't you think that would have seemed a little strange? I mean we aren't supposed to be that buddy-buddy. I knew she'd tell you. Where is she now?"

"She's lying down. That news about the insurance really took its toll on her. She's on tranquilizers, and they pretty well knock her out."

"She has a right to be upset. I love her dearly, but that was a stupid thing to do. One more motive on the cops' list."

"Tommi, I need to talk to you. How can we meet without raising any eyebrows?"

"I've got to meet a claims adjuster at my place at three. Why don't you tell Daniel and Nina that I could use your advice so you're going to meet me there."

"Perfect. I'll do that. See you soon."

I had about an hour-and-a-half before I needed to be at the condominium. I found the notes that I had taken during my research at the library and looked them over. There was one couple, Devon and Ginger Carmichael, whose names appeared every time along with Nina and Cap's in the society columns. When I looked them up in the telephone book, I had found, unsurprisingly, that they lived in one of the most exclusive sections of town. I dialed their number and when Mrs. Carmichael answered, explained who I was. Ginger invited me to come out to the house right away. "I've been so upset about Nina and Cap, I'd like to do anything I can to help her."

The Carmichaels lived in the Irving Park area of town which was the oldest, most established of the wealthy neighborhoods. The curving streets were shaded by mature oaks and sycamores that had been planted when the area was developed just after the depression. Sheltered under the towering trees were hundreds of dogwoods and redbuds that gave a fairyland effect in the spring when in full bloom. Now, in a few weeks, the area would be a kaleidoscope of brilliant fall color.

The Carmichael house was a huge Tudor-style home with wings and gables everywhere set on a lawn so perfect and without blemish it resembled artificial turf. A new Cadillac Escalade sat in the driveway, dwarfing my car when I pulled in behind it.

A slender blonde in white linen slacks and jade green silk blouse answered my knock at the front door. I had almost expected a maid in uniform, but I guess, though the rich still have plenty of help, it's not quite so much in evidence these days. Cleaning and landscaping services take the place of personal staff. "Mrs. Poag?" she said, "I'm Ginger. Come on in." She led me into her living room which was almost, though not quite, as elegant as Nina's. It had the self-consciously cluttered look of an English drawing room. We each sat on matching chairs covered in a chintz rampant with pink roses.

"How is Nina?" was the first thing Ginger said.

"She's doing pretty well, considering," I answered.

"Poor thing. I feel so sorry for her."

"Me too. That's why I'm trying to see if I can help her. I hoped her friends could tell me things that the police wouldn't know about. I mean there's got to be some explanation other than saying Nina did it."

"Of course she didn't do it. What can I tell you?" Maybe Nina had felt uncomfortable around the women she socialized with, but Ginger seemed genuinely concerned about her. If Nina hadn't had such low self esteem, she might have been more able to accept and enjoy their friendship.

"What was Cap like? I never had a chance to meet him," I asked

Ginger became thoughtful. "Cap was the personification of Hollywood: party lover, big spender, big drinker, outrageous flirt. The women kind of enjoyed it when he hit on them. We all took it as a lark; nobody took him seriously. The men seemed both attracted and repelled. They admired him for his success and envied his talent and connections. On the other hand, they hated it when he flirted so shamelessly with their wives."

"Do you think anyone hated him enough to kill him or have him killed?"

"I'm sure there wasn't anyone like that in our group. The husbands might not have liked his flirtations, but most of them aren't entirely innocent themselves. Just more discreet. Besides, what Cap did with the local women was harmless. I'm pretty sure he wasn't having any affairs here in town. A few of us knew about this Allison, but she's apparently not from around here."

"Do you know if she's in New York?"

"Nina once told me that. But I overheard something Cap said to my husband the last time we were together. He said, 'Nina thinks I'm going to New York next week,' and gave Devon a meaningful wink that indicated he wasn't going to New York at all, and he sure wasn't going to attend to business. I didn't have the heart to tell Nina because I knew the subject hurt her so much."

"Did he give any indication at all where he *was* going?"

"No, he played it very cool. He always reminded me of a high school kid who tried to present himself as quite the Don Juan, the Hugh Hefner of central North Carolina. I never could understand what Nina saw in him. She's a dear sweet thing, but she's also insecure. And that enabled him to walk all over her."

"Do you know of anyone else who might know anything about this Allison?"

Ginger chewed on her lip as she contemplated this.. "You know, Alice Jeffries works with the North Carolina Film Commission. It's possible she might have heard something since she works with the industry." She went to the beautiful antique secretary for Alice's address and phone number and wrote it down on a card for me. I thanked her and left to meet Frank and the adjuster at the condominium.

So Allison didn't live in New York. I wondered why Daniel was so convinced that she did.

Chapter
eighteen

Both the insurance adjuster and Frank were there when I arrived, Frank in Nina's BMW. As soon as I pulled up, they got out and followed me into the house, all of us bracing ourselves against the pungent odor. The back of the house was dark because the sliding door and window had been boarded up. While the men examined the burned-out laundry room, I went upstairs to pack more clothes into large trash bags, wondering if the smell would ever come out of them.

When the adjuster, Albert Cochran, had finished his inspection, he suggested we go to the patio to discuss his findings. As I passed through the gate in the fence, I suddenly saw Tee huddled in the far corner. I cried out his name and ran over and gathered him up. "Oh, Tee, you're back." I cuddled him in my arms and could feel him trembling. My mood brightened immeasurably. Now that I'd found Tee, I felt could deal with my other problems. What's a burned out laundry room when I had my bosom buddy back.

Cochran walked over and petted him. "So this is the infamous cat, is it?"

"I'd say he's been falsely accused, but I can't prove it. Before we start, let me feed him. He must be starved since he ran away after the fire." I fixed him a heaping bowl of his favorite Ocean Bouquet, hardly noticing its foul smell as I dished it up in the greater stench of the house, and a large bowl of water. Out on the patio, Tee lit into it with an urgency far beyond his usual keenness to eat.

With Tee taken care of, we began the discussion. Cochran named a sum that would include all repairs, cleaning and painting the rest of the condo, replacing the downstairs carpet, kitchen floor and any furniture destroyed by smoke and/or water, and my motel bills while the work was being done. It sounded very fair to me. I was so elated at finding Tee that I probably would have agreed to anything.

Frank was quiet the entire time, but I suspected he might have put in a word or two in my favor while the men were alone. He seemed to understand my need to make my own decisions. It had been hard after the divorce; I was accustomed to Bernard taking charge. I knew I'd been a victim of my generation and its attitudes. And I soon discovered it was a heady experience to choose my own path, regardless of the outcome. Frank, it seemed, had sensed this intuitively. Or, miracle of miracles, perhaps he was one of those rare men who had always assumed women were as capable as he was.

After the adjuster left, I told Frank I wanted to pack the car with clothes and other items I needed to take to the motel. I shut Tee in the spare bedroom as he helped me carry out the bags filled with clothes, boxes with personal papers, the microwave and coffee maker, after I wiped the layers of soot off of them..

When we were ready to leave, I retrieved Tee and put him in the back seat of the car along with piles of shoes and extra hangers and boxes filled with the contents of my medicine cabinet and my jewelry.

Frank followed me to the motel in Nina's car and helped me unload everything. Tee, confined to the bathroom while this was happening, explored the motel room with wariness once he was let out, sniffing and rubbing the furniture to mark this place as his own.

Frank and I sat on separate beds to talk. I described my escape from the burning house, which unfortunately made me relive the terror once again. I repeated the fireman's conclusion about how the fire was started, and shared my misgivings with him.

"I'm worried about you, Tommi," he said. "I don't like the sound of it at all." He moved over to my bed and took my good hand in his. "It's pure selfishness on my part, but it's the first time since Marilyn died that I've enjoyed anyone's company so much. I just don't want anything to happen to you."

I felt uncomfortable. "Time heals, you know. I think you've simply gotten to the point where you can enjoy life again. I have nothing to do with that," I told him. This kind of flattery was foreign to me. I thought his eagerness to work with me was solely for Nina's benefit, but maybe I was as insecure as Nina. I'm good at analyzing others, but it might be worth it to take a good hard look at myself.

"No, no, there's more to it than that. Having been a widower for several years, I've met lots of women, believe me. They come out of the woodwork when you're a single man again. But I've never felt so comfortable around any of them as I have around you."

I squeezed Frank's hand and then let go. "Frank, we've got to concentrate on one thing at a time. And right now, that's Nina's defense. You're very sweet. But let's not get side-tracked."

I was amazed to see his face redden. "Of course that's my first priority. But your safety is connected with that, and I couldn't forgive myself if anything happened to you."

"Nothing's going to happen," I replied with more conviction than I felt. "Now let me tell you what else I've done." I told him about my visits with Robert Truesdale and Ginger Carmichael. Frank listened intently.

"So Truesdale could have been at Lake Brandt that night since he can't prove he was at the beach," he said when I finished.

"He could have been. But he would have to be an awfully good actor to seem so convincing when he talked about Cap as if he were alive." Now I was playing Devil's advocate. I couldn't make up my mind about Robby.

"But it *is* possible he pushed the car in."

"Sure, it's possible."

"What do you make of Mrs. Carmichael's statement, that Allison might not live in New York?" he asked.

"I was quite surprised. Both Nina and Daniel seemed convinced she lives there."

"I feel so frustrated over this Allison thing," Frank said. "We're never going to track her down."

"I've got an idea on that. Would it be possible to get Daniel and Nina out of the house at the same time? Couldn't we go through Cap's papers, tax forms, things like that, and see if we can't find something that would point to her?"

"Of course! I should have thought of that. And I wouldn't be intruding into Nina's privacy since she's asked me to help her with the estate when she's given the go-ahead on it. Nina has an appointment with Bernard tomorrow afternoon. And Daniel has volunteered to drive her there because he needs to do some business in town. That would be the perfect opportunity. Come on out around 1:30. They'll be leaving a little after one. And if you happened to be there when they return, we can just say you were concerned about Nina and came out to see her."

"Great. Maybe we'll be able to find something that will point us in the right direction at last. By the way, did you get in touch with Ernie Zaleski?"

"He is obnoxious, isn't he? It didn't take much imagination to know how he'd be with women. Anyway, he didn't tell me much except that he met with Morgan Proxmire late in the afternoon the day Cap died, so that gives them a mutual alibi. Actually, Proxmire was trying to find out what recourse he might have if Cap fired him. He knew Zaleski couldn't represent him since he was Cap's lawyer. But the two of them had become friends over the years so he wanted to get a feel of what was going on with Cap. But, anyway, they were in Hollywood on the twelfth."

"Couldn't Proxmire have flown out here after their meeting and done it?" Was I now grasping at straws?

"Maybe if he'd been flying west because you gain three hours, but flying east you lose three, so it would have been next to impossible." Frank had probably done much more flying than I had. I'd forgotten about the time zones.

"He could have hired someone." After I said it, it occurred to me that maybe I'd seen too many gangster movies.

"True, but I very much doubt it. Even though he had reason to despise Cap, his main concern was losing a big source of his income if Cap dumped him. It wouldn't have made sense for Morgan to kill the guy."

"What else did Ernie say?"

"Something that I had suspected. Cap had been hiding his assets, sending them down to the Caribbean and trying to hold off divorcing Nina till he could get most of it stashed away. But in recent weeks he'd quit doing that. Zaleski wasn't sure why. Cap never told him much about his private life unless he needed legal advice on it. But he wondered if it meant that Cap was reconsidering his plans to leave Nina."

"So, if the police know that Cap was transferring his money, that would give them even more reason to suspect Nina. They'd think she meant to kill him before he could cheat her out of a good divorce settlement."

Frank shook his head glumly. "It keeps adding up against her." He stood up. "Well, not much we can do now till tomorrow afternoon. How about some dinner, Tommi?"

"To tell you the truth, I'm exhausted," I said. "I didn't sleep at all last night and it has caught up with me. Think I'll just fall into bed."

"You get some rest then, and I'll see you tomorrow afternoon."

When I rose to see him out, he put his hands on my shoulders and leaned down and gave me a brief kiss, then hugged me tightly. Letting go he said, "You take care of yourself. Don't take any unnecessary chances." Before I could reply, he was out the door.

It had been such a long time since I'd been embraced by a man. The warmth lasted all the while I bathed and brushed my teeth and got ready for bed. I couldn't decide whether it was simply the good feeling of the hug that lingered so long or because it was Frank.

But I was too tired to reach any conclusion. I fell quickly into a deep sleep and woke only briefly a couple of times when Tee walked around the bed trying to find a familiar spot to curl up in. He'd actually created a small depression for himself on my bed at home, but there was none to be found on this super-firm mattress. I hoped we both would get used to our new home quickly. But maybe we were both too old to make an easy adjustment.

Chapter
nineteen

I could hardly believe it was morning when I awoke to the sun filtering around the edge of the dark green drapes. I was starved after skipping supper. First off I'd go get a doughnut and coffee before buying a couple of TV dinners to stash in the tiny freezer compartment of the refrigerator along with some Cokes and milk and orange juice. I'd have to shop every couple of days, but that was no great burden having done mostly pickup shopping for the past year.

After returning with my groceries, I busied myself hanging up the clothes I'd brought from home the day before. I'd found only a few things in clothing bags or in drawers that didn't stink of smoke. The rest would have to go to the cleaners. With such limited space, I'd have to keep everything well organized to get through these next weeks with a modicum of equanimity. I was putting my jewelry in a night stand drawer when the phone rang.

"Tommi? It's Michelle."

That was a surprise. I'd never expected her to call me. Once the funeral was over, I figured it was out of sight, out of mind.

"Hi. How are you?"

"The question is how are *you*? I heard about the fire from Dad." So that explained it.

"I'm all in one piece. That's the important thing."

"Thank God for that. Tommi, I need to talk with you. Could you meet me for lunch today?" I thought it had been a half-hearted attempt to be gracious when she said we ought to get together sometime.

"Providing it's early enough," I told her. "I have a 1:30 appointment."

"How about noon at Panda Inn in Friendly Shopping Center. That's close to work for me."

"Good enough." I was really curious as to what this was about. But I wasn't thrilled at the idea of being with her again.

I had just enough time to call a couple of contractors and make arrangements to meet them at my condo that evening, one at seven-thirty and one at nine, before it was time to leave.

I was the first one to arrive at the restaurant, but Michelle came along shortly. We both decided to have the buffet lunch and loaded our plates with everything from egg rolls to moo goo gai pan.

Michelle ate with considerable relish, using chopsticks clumsily. I knew better than to even try.

"I'm real concerned about Dad." Michelle finally stopped eating long enough to get to the point of the meeting.

"Why?"

"I was at Nina's last night. She was out in the yard when the phone rang so I answered it. I hadn't realized Dad was in the other room, and he picked up the phone at the same time I did." She took another bite, and I waited impatiently while she chewed. "He answered before I had a chance, and I was about to hang up when I heard this rough voice, so I stayed on the line to listen. Someone was threatening him, Tommi! They told him to keep his nose out of things or he'd be sorry. It was real scary. I figured it was useless to ask him about it. He'd just brush it off and say it was somebody's idea of a sick joke. But I don't think it was. I think the guy was dead serious. I'm worried sick over him."

"You're sure it was for real?" I was going to try and dissuade her from taking it seriously. Michelle had no reason to believe that Frank was involved in any way. But I felt a cold chill. Now I knew how Frank felt when he thought I was in danger.

"Oh, definitely. Dad told me earlier the two of you were trying to help Nina, and I think you've stirred up a hornet's nest. Look, Tommi, I don't want anything to happen to Dad. I lost Mom at a young age. I don't want to lose him too. You've got to get him to stop this before something awful happens."

Damn it all. Why did Frank have to spill his guts to Michelle? I only hoped she didn't decide to tell Nina. That would really blow the roof off of things, and we didn't need more complications. And how serious was this threat? Taken together with the fire, I had to admit I was very concerned, but I didn't want Michelle to know that. It was important to reassure her.

"I'll talk to him, Michelle, though I'm afraid he's determined to do this. Anyway, it probably *was* just a crank call. Besides, we haven't found out anything substantial. It's not like we're on the verge of solving the case, and I don't think anyone would believe that we are."

"Why don't you stop while you're ahead and let the police do their job. That's what we pay them for. I don't want you and Dad getting yourselves hurt. That isn't going to help Nina."

"The cops are so sure she's guilty, they aren't even looking anywhere else. Look, I'll talk to your dad and convince him that we need to be extra careful. I'm sure he will be cautious for your sake even if he's not concerned about himself."

Michelle looked disappointed. "That's it? Just ask him to be careful? Can't you talk him into getting out of it, period?"

I shook my head. I did feel sorry for Michelle. Her mother had died, her sister was accused of killing her husband, and now she perceived that her father was in danger. That would be a terrible burden for anyone. "He's pretty determined, Michelle. But I'll do what I can."

By the time we parted, Michelle was barely speaking, overcome by depression.

I had tried to steer the conversation toward lighter subjects, but Michelle would have none of it. Finally, we finished our meals in silence, Michelle forlornly trying to pick up the last bits of food with her chopsticks, while I was left wondering if she was going to make our lives miserable until she got her way. How I wished Frank had kept his mouth shut. But it was natural to want to include Michelle. He probably thought she could help. Fat chance! I suspected Michelle would be on Frank's case every chance she got. She was just going to make our job more difficult.

Michelle left to return to work and I drove to Oak Ridge. It was another hot September day, the sun unchallenged in the cerulean sky. I looked forward to October when the temperatures would moderate, and the days would have that crisp, tangy feel to them. I always wanted to bottle those days so I could pull them out and experience them on the hottest, most humid days of July or the overcast, bone-chilling days of February.

I reached the Sellars' house a little after one-thirty, and Frank answered my knock almost immediately. As always, we went to the family room, bypassing the formal living room.

"Look, before we start, Frank, we've got to discuss something," I said as I sat on one of the white sofas. "I just had lunch with Michelle, and she's very upset. Did you get a threatening call last night?"

Frank looked shocked. "Good Lord, how did she know about it?"

"She picked up the phone the same time you did and overheard the conversation. She said you'd told her about our investigation, and she asked me to convince you to drop it. Didn't you realize how much it would upset her?"

"She wasn't upset when I explained to her what we were doing. Of course I made it seem pretty innocuous. I suppose I shouldn't have said anything, but when she asked me why you'd driven all the way to Reidsville to see her, I said you were probably just doing some background checking on Cap. That we both thought the cops had gotten it wrong. It had to be the phone call that got her all riled up."

I rubbed my nose thoughtfully. "I suppose you're right. What about this call? Do you think it's a serious threat? Is it something we should report to the police?"

"How are we going to do that? We sure as heck can't tell them we're investigating Nina's case. And otherwise they'll just say it was some kid dialing randomly trying to scare the bejesus out of people."

"What can we do about it then?"

"Be damn careful."

"What about Michelle? What are you going to tell her?"

"I'll probably tell her she's right and I've quit looking into it just to relieve her mind. I'm not proud of having to lie to my own daughter, but I don't want her making herself sick with worry."

"Well, for that and many other reasons I wish we could come up with something quickly—like yesterday."

"You said the magic words. Let's start looking through Cap's papers." He left the room and came back several minutes later carrying two cardboard file boxes. "I haven't been able to go through any of this yet with Nina in the house. So we've got to hustle." He set them on the floor beside the sofa and opened the top one revealing several large manila envelopes. Each held one year's tax records.

"Let's start with last year's," Frank said, pulling the contents of the envelope out onto the coffee table made from an old sea chest. I moved the Mexican clay cat to a side table to make room so we could spread out the contents.

Frank handed me a stack of papers and took another stack for himself. I found receipts for gifts to charitable foundations, medical bills, property-tax bills, and documentation for a room Cap rented in a small office condo in Oak Ridge. That was probably where he did his writing. But nothing of any help to us.

"Look," Frank said, handing me a sheet of paper, "Here's a bill from Bingham

Travel Agency. It covers the last three months of last year. Nothing to indicate he'd made any trips except to the expected places."

I scrutinized the statement. There was one trip to New York, three to L.A. and that was all. "Maybe we need to find a bill from the time when he still lived in California," I said. "If Allison *is* in New York, he wasn't seeing her much. Wonder if she was meeting him in L.A.? Or maybe she was *from* L.A. But then why would he move here? Just to make sure Nina wouldn't catch them together?"

Frank searched through the cardboard box and pulled out an envelope for a year earlier. This time he thumbed quickly through its contents, pulling out some papers stapled together. "Here's what we're looking for," he said.

This time the bills were from a Los Angeles travel agency, Sunshine Travel. Altogether there were five trips to New York for the year, not exactly a schedule to indicate a passionate romance, and several to Greensboro.

"What do you make of these trips to Greensboro?" I asked.

"It had to be that he was house hunting."

"Oh, right. I'm surprised it took him so long to find this one."

"You've got to understand Cap. No ordinary place would do. He'd have a hard time finding something up to his standards. If anyone ever wanted to outdo the Joneses, Cap was the man."

"Nina said he was very picky. What about phone records? Where are they?"

Frank leafed through the documents he was holding without results. I found no phone bills in my envelope either.

"Doesn't make sense," Frank said. "He would have taken his business calls off his income tax."

"Maybe he didn't think it was worth the risk of having Nina see them."

"Of course. He was probably calling Allison often. The mere fact they're missing is the most significant thing we've found yet." Frank sounded excited.

"Don't they use ACS phone service? Undoubtedly dear old dad sold them on doing that."

"Of course I did. I'll call the home office and have them fax me a copy of his records. Nina mentioned that Cap had a fax machine at his rented office, and I know where the key is. Let's go over there right now."

"Why don't I stay here and clean up this stuff," I said indicating the tax records strewn across the sofa and coffee table. "Then if Nina and Daniel get back before you do, I'll make up some excuse for you."

"Tell them that I needed to buy some clothing. I only brought a carry-on when I came. I'll pick up a shirt or two to make it look legit."

"And I'll say I came to see Nina and caught you just as you were leaving. So I decided to sit on the patio and wait for her because it was such a beautiful day."

We did a high five together.

Frank laughed. "We're getting too good at this stuff, Tommi. What a pair of liars we've turned out to be."

"I know. And isn't it fun when you're doing it for a good cause?"

"I don't know about the fun part. The fire at your place wouldn't qualify." Frank's smile had vanished.

That sobered me. "That wasn't fun at all. Take my word for it."

He showed me where to put the file boxes and left for Cap's office.

Chapter
twenty

Almost an hour later, before Frank had returned, Nina and Daniel came home. I had been sitting on the patio enjoying the glorious day, watching the squirrels scampering up and down the huge pin oaks that surrounded the house. I needed the break. I'd been feeling pretty frenetic about my "investigative work" as though Nina's life depended upon my success. And maybe it did.

"Well, hi," Nina said as she came out onto the patio from the family room. "I saw your car out front. What a nice surprise." She seemed pale and wan, and though she was trying to be upbeat, her voice lacked its usual vivacity.

"I should have called first. But it was such a pretty day I thought I'd just drive on over."

"Where's Dad?"

"He said he needed to pick up some shirts or something. He was a little light on the luggage when he came. How are you doing, Nina?"

Nina dropped into a chair beside me. "Not good. Bernard tries to encourage me, but I can tell he's real worried."

"I'm sure he has everything well under control." I hated myself when I spouted such guff, but I had to keep encouraging her. Frank and I had vowed to be her personal pep squad, doing everything we could to counter her depression.

"He's doing a terrific job, really," Nina sounded as if she were trying to convince herself. "It's just that there are so many things against me. I don't know how much he can do."

I was so worried about her. She seemed to have lost any spark of hope she once had. "I'm sure it's going to turn out okay. You're innocent, Nina, and you're going to beat this thing."

Nina stood up, tears gathering in her eyes. "Will you excuse me Tommi? I need to go up and lie down. I'm sorry to be such a rotten hostess." And she ran into the house.

I suspected that Nina was medicating herself into oblivion to avoid the reality of her situation. If this continued, she'd either become hooked on barbiturates or accidentally take too many. I hoped Frank was keeping a very close eye on her.

Daniel came out onto the patio from the kitchen door. "Well hello, Tommi, how are you? What's wrong with Nina? I saw her running up the stairs."

"I think she's feeling very desperate. Did she tell you what Bernard said today? I thought maybe that's why she is so upset."

"No, she didn't talk at all. She seemed very withdrawn." He sat in one of the chairs he pulled out from the small table where Nina and I had lunch the first time I came here.

"I hate the thought of you and Frank going home. No telling what she'd do if she were alone."

"Frank had better stay on for a while. She needs him now more than ever. By the way, where is he?"

"At the store. He should be back shortly."

"How about a beer? I feel the need for one." He was already up, on his way to the kitchen.

"Just the ticket." I said.

Daniel brought me a beer in a frosted mug and one for himself, and we sat on the patio chatting and trying to enjoy the day. He asked about the fire and frowned and shook his head sympathetically as I described the damage it had wrought on my condo. I described my funky motel to him.

"So you're pretending to be camping out?" he asked. "You must have a vivid imagination to be able to convince yourself you're in the woods."

I laughed. "When you're desperate, you'll go to great lengths to tolerate your situation."

It wasn't long before Frank came out on the patio to join us, carrying a beer. We talked about the football season, politics, and which nearby town had the best barbeque, just long enough to make it seem like a casual visit.

Finally I stood to go. "I guess I'd better get home before I get caught in rush hour traffic."

"Let me walk you to your car," Frank said, and we walked around the house to my Mitsubishi which was parked on the curved drive.

"Well?" I asked when we were out of earshot of Daniel.

"Never fails. The computer was down. But they thought it would be up first thing tomorrow, so I'll try again."

When I got back to the motel, Tee was a real pest, mewing continuously and rubbing my legs furiously. I noticed that his food bowl was empty and realized I'd forgotten to feed him that morning. Poor baby. I opened a can and spooned the contents into his dish, then microwaved myself a frozen spaghetti dinner as he gobbled his meal down. I poured a Coke and wished I had some wine instead. Coke and spaghetti—ugh.

What I needed was a nice hot soothing bath. I ran the water almost to the top, a treat because my small water heater at home was not adequate to fill the tub. Now I could indulge myself. Small compensation for having to live here, but I tried to think positive.

I stepped into the tub and eased myself down against its sloping back.

Immediately my tenseness began to drain away, leaving me feeling relaxed and sleepy. In fact, I suddenly was very tired, as if weights were in my limbs, pulling at them like a double dose of gravity. I didn't know why I would be this exhausted. I'd slept much longer than usual last night and by this morning had regained much of my energy. But now this terrible fatigue was sapping my strength, making me lightheaded. I was afraid that at this rate I might fall asleep and slip under the water. I had to get to my bed.

My limbs were so weak it seemed as if I were climbing a mountain just to pull myself out of the bathtub. What was happening to me? I knew I had to call someone for help. I was getting sicker by the minute. I stumbled out of the bathroom and headed clumsily toward the nearest bed, every step a monumental effort. The phone on the night stand was so far away, so impossibly far away. I somehow managed to reach the side of the bed and started to pull myself across the coverlet when everything went dark.

I heard someone calling my name. I opened my eyes and saw Frank leaning over me. Anxiety drew furrows in his forehead and tight lines around his mouth. Where on earth was I? I was confused, disoriented. I looked around and saw that I was in a bed enclosed by curtains. A hospital. I was in a hospital!

"Tommi, thank God you're okay." Frank was holding my hand tightly.

"What's going on?" I closed my eyes momentarily, trying to force a memory, something to explain why I was here. I vaguely remembered being in the bathtub and suddenly feeling as if every ounce of vitality was being drained from me. I called up fuzzy memories of struggling to reach the bed where I must have passed out. "Did I have a stroke?" That possibility was always in the back of my mind since my mother died of a stroke at age 68. I checked my arms and legs to make sure they moved. They all did.

"No, they think you ate or drank something, though they haven't analyzed the contents of your stomach yet."

"You mean they pumped it?"

"Sure did."

How gross I thought, thankful I wasn't awake when they did it.

"My gosh, Frank, tell me what happened."

"I called to tell you I got another one of those threatening calls. But you didn't answer your phone. You'd told me you were going straight home, and with all the things that have been going on, I was sure something had happened to you. I did about 85 getting here, surprised a cop didn't stop me. When you didn't answer the door even though your car was out front, I got the manager to let me in."

I covered my face with my hands in embarrassment. "Oh, Frank, that isn't exactly the image of me I wanted you to remember—in the buff, that is."

He gently pushed back a stray lock on my forehead. "Just thank the good Lord that I came when I did." He leaned over and kissed me on the cheek.

I closed my eyes. I didn't feel so sick now, but I had no energy. Whatever happened had robbed me of my strength.

I heard Frank whisper, "You go to sleep now."

I woke up again when they brought in a food tray. When the aide lifted the cover, a meal of broth, crackers, Jell-O and tea was revealed. I was so hungry now I couldn't believe they'd only bring me this pitiful stuff. Frank was still sitting beside me. "One of Cone Hospital's famous gourmet meals, I see," he said with a teasing smile.

"I don't suppose you'd sneak me in a hamburger," I pleaded.

"If you'll answer a couple of questions first."

I made a face to indicate what choice do I have?

"What did you eat or drink this afternoon?"

"Chinese buffet at noon, a beer with Daniel, and a Coke and frozen spaghetti dinner back in my room."

"Daniel? You know, we haven't given too much thought to him. Did he and Cap have any problems?"

I pushed myself up a little in the bed. "Nina said that they fought off and on. But Daniel denied it when I asked him."

Frank rubbed his jaw thoughtfully. "Did anybody ever ask Daniel where he was when Cap died?"

"No. I assumed he was in New York."

"I think I need to go have a talk with Daniel. Maybe I should go right now. You'll be safe enough here. They're planning on keeping you overnight for observation."

"Go get me a hamburger first, won't you?" I pleaded.

"And if I don't?" He raised his eyebrows, pretending to give me a hard time.

"I'll sic Bernard on you."

"Anything but that," Frank said, throwing up his arms in surrender. "There's a Burger King a few blocks away. I won't be long."

"Oh, and would you mind calling the contractors who were coming over tonight and canceling them? I've got their numbers in my purse." I looked around the room. "Do I have a purse? Seems I was a little underdressed when you found me."

"In the drawer there," Frank pointed to the night stand. "And luckily I had the presence of mind to get the clothes from your bathroom and pack them in a paper bag for you. They're in the closet. But it's too late to call the contractors. They'd have come and gone by now. You or I can call them tomorrow and explain what happened."

"Oh, darn," I said.

Frank left, promising to return shortly. As soon as he was gone, I rang for the nurse. A pleasant dark-haired young woman answered my call.

"You're looking pretty chipper," she said.

"Who's my doctor?" I asked.

"Dr. Kowicki."

"Is he still in the hospital?"

"Yes, in fact he's on the floor."

"Could you ask him to come see me?"

"Sure. I'll send him 'round."

Dr. Kowicki was there in about ten minutes. It made me wonder whether I was that sick or the hospital just had a light caseload. The doctor examined me carefully and asked how I felt. I summoned up all my resources and told him with a smile that I was just great, thanks, which was a fairly sizable exaggeration. But I'd certainly also felt much worse in my life. And I was sure that I would be perfectly normal by the next day.

"I want to be discharged, doctor," I told him.

"I'd planned to keep you overnight for observation." He was writing on my chart as he spoke.

"I have something very urgent I must do this evening. Can't you let me check back with you tomorrow? It's terribly important to me." Lies, lies, how easily they came.

He swung his stethoscope slowly back and forth as he contemplated my request. "It's really against my better judgment, but you seem to be doing well. I'll have the nurse make an appointment for you to see me tomorrow, and I'll leave your release at the nurses' station."

As soon as he left the room, I got the bag of clothes out of the closet and went into the bathroom to dress. I was sitting in the green vinyl chair beside the bed when Frank returned with a bag full of carry-out food.

He scowled when he saw me. "What's this?" he asked. "You're not going anywhere, Tommi."

"Oh, yes, the doctor says I can."

"What did you do? Torture him with Jell-O and bouillon?"

"Give me that," I demanded, snatching the bag from his hand. I emptied its contents onto the rolling bed table. Holding up the container of french fries, I said, "Here, have some. We're going to need our strength if we're going to wheedle the truth out of Daniel."

"What do you mean 'we'?"

"I mean I'm coming with you. We're a team, remember? Besides *I* was the one who ate or drank something nasty, and I want to know who gave it to me."

Chapter
twenty-one

I soon realized I was unsteady on my feet, but I wasn't about to let Frank know. I walked to the nurses' station with as much zest as I could muster. The nurses insisted that I be taken to the car in a wheelchair—hospital policy, you know—and I didn't protest at all. They handed me a card noting that I was to see the doctor at 9:30 the next morning.

Frank drove Nina's BMW up to the hospital door where the aide had pushed my chair. On the way out of town we discussed the best way to broach the subject of Cap and Daniel's relationship. Should we confront him in front of Nina to witness his reaction to her allegations that the brothers had fought, or should we leave her out of it considering her fragile mental health?

"I don't think you should include Nina," I said. "She's got about all she can handle. Let's just ask him point blank and watch him squirm."

"She was knocked out when I left the house anyway. She's probably still asleep."

"I'm really worried about that, Frank. I think she's taking entirely too much medication. Now that I think about it, there's probably a lot of sleeping pills floating around that house. Daniel wouldn't have had a problem getting his hands on some."

"He sure wouldn't. Nina's doctor has been very generous with the prescriptions. I suppose that's typical treatment for grieving wives."

"What about those threatening phone calls, Frank? Was Daniel in the room when you got them?"

He thought a minute. "No."

"So he could have made them from another phone in the house. Cap had a separate business line there." My mind was dancing around the various possibilities.

"You're absolutely right. Maybe we should have been looking into Daniel more carefully from the start."

"But who would think of his brother!"

"You have heard of Cain and Abel haven't you?"

We rode in silence the rest of the way, brooding over what all this could mean.

It was almost ten o'clock by the time we pulled into the driveway of Nina's house. The downstairs windows were brightly lit, giving the house a warm, welcoming appearance. Frank unlocked the door, and I followed him inside.

"Daniel must be in the family room watching TV," Frank said. "I think there's an exhibition game on tonight."

I led the way through the kitchen to the family room and stopped short just inside the doorway. "Oh, no!" I exclaimed. Daniel lay on the floor wedged between the sofa and the coffee table. The television was on and a nearly empty glass of beer and a bowl of popcorn were on the end table.

Frank had to half climb over the coffee table to reach Daniel's wrist to feel his pulse. It appeared as though he'd been sitting on the sofa and had fallen forward when he was stricken. There was a large discolored lump at the side of his forehead indicating that he might have struck his head on the corner of the table as he fell. Or someone could have hit him with a blunt object. Frank looked up at me and shook his head. "Nothing."

I was stunned. I'd never expected this. "We need to call the police. My God, this is a nightmare."

"Before we do anything, I've got to check on Nina." Frank jumped up and ran as I followed him up the stairs and into Nina's bedroom. He turned on the light to reveal Nina apparently sound asleep. He shook her by the shoulders. "Nina!" His voice was anxious.

She opened her eyes, looked at us groggily, then sat up in bed, startled. "What's the matter?"

He sat down beside her and took her hand. "Thank God you're okay. It's Daniel. He's dead."

"What!" Nina's eyes were round as saucers and full of fear. Her whole body began to shake.

"Tommi and I just came in and found him on the family room floor. When did you last see him, Nina?"

"Just after we got back from Greensboro. I've been in bed since I left Tommi on the patio. What time is it?"

"Ten o'clock. Did you hear anything?"

"I took a pill when I came upstairs and it knocked me right out. Oh Dad, what happened to him?"

"We don't know," I said. "Maybe he had a heart attack." Frank gave me a funny look, but why give Nina the worst possible scenario? I didn't intend to tell her about my own close call; Nina couldn't take much more. "We need to call the police now. You want me to stay with you while Frank calls them?"

"I've got to get some clothes on. You go on. I'm going to take a quick shower. I feel hung over." She swung her legs over the side of the bed and struggled to get up. I wanted to help her to the bathroom, but I knew she didn't want to appear helpless. So I went back downstairs with Frank.

"I'm dialing 911," Frank said. "This is really going to open a can of worms, but I don't have a choice."

After speaking with the dispatcher, he hung up and wrung his hands. "It's the sheriff's deputy that's coming. There's no police department in this town. I guess there's nothing we can do but wait."

I didn't want to be in the family room with Daniel's body so we sat at the breakfast table. I was beginning to wish I'd stayed in the hospital as Frank had wanted me to.

"What do you think?" he asked me as he drummed on the table with his fingers; it was the slow cadence of a funeral march.

"I just don't know," I said despondently. "I was beginning to think that Daniel had something to do with Cap's death, but that theory doesn't jibe now."

"It's possible it could have been a natural cause like you said."

"I said that for Nina's sake. You don't really believe that, do you?"

"Well, why would anyone want to kill him?" Frank picked up the salt shaker and began to roll it back and forth between his palms. "It doesn't make sense."

Neither of us spoke for a few minutes, both deep in our own thoughts. Finally I, testing a theory out loud, said, "This is really a far-out idea. But what if he killed himself in remorse after trying to murder me? Let's say he could rationalize murdering Cap because he thought of him as a rotten brother who deserved to die. We don't know what he had against him, but Cap told Nina they had serious arguments. Daniel was afraid we'd figure out he did it, so he wanted to get rid of us too."

"But Tommi, how would he know we were investigating?"

"Michelle could have told him when she was here. She seemed pretty obsessed with the idea that we were involved and could have complained to Daniel."

"Pretty far-fetched. But go on," Frank said.

"He had a chance to doctor my beer, but not yours. Only before he could do something to you, he became overwhelmed with guilt over my 'demise' since I hadn't hurt him in any way. So he took whatever he gave me and killed himself. And as he lost consciousness and fell over, he hit his head on the coffee table accounting for the lump on his head."

"I think I follow you. And I'm not sure I share your thinking on it. But stranger things have happened, I guess."

"How about this? Daniel was Allison's lover before Cap. After all, he lived in New York. He killed Cap out of jealousy."

"It took him a long time to get around to it then."

"Maybe he was the slow burn type."

"After that long, I'd say it's more like burnt out. I don't know, Tommi. I don't figure him as the killer."

"Me either. Just going through the 'what if?' routine trying not to overlook any possibility."

Just then we heard a siren and both of us went to the front door.

A big man, tall and husky and built like a pro football player, stood on the porch. "Deputy Switzer," he said, extending his hand.

We led him into the family room where he felt Daniel's carotid artery. "Looks like he might have been dead a while," he said. "Getting a little stiff. Tell me what you know."

Frank explained how we found him.

"The two of you had just come in? Was anyone else in the house when you arrived?"

This was the question I had dreaded. My heart began beating faster.

"Yes," said Frank. "My daughter was upstairs asleep."

"Oh? And where is she now?"

"She's getting dressed. She should be down in a minute."

The deputy nodded his head thoughtfully. "You two," he said, "why did you come here?"

"We were...," Frank began. I elbowed him in the ribs.

"Frank, Mr. Poag here, has been staying with his daughter, but he went into Greensboro early this evening to visit me. He's concerned about his daughter, Nina, and came to talk to me about her. He knew she was taking sleeping pills, and in fact she was heavily sedated when he left. That's why I came back with him—to check on her. We found her sound asleep in bed just where he left her several hours ago."

"And who is this gentleman?" Switzer asked, indicating Daniel.

"That is my daughter's brother-in-law, Daniel Sellars," Frank replied.

Switzer's face registered recognition. "Oh, yes, Sellars. The Oscar Sellars' death. I believe your daughter was arrested for his murder. Right?" Waiting for an answer, he looked Frank steadily in the eye.

"Yes, sir." The color was beginning to drain from Frank's face. This was like a nightmare we couldn't escape.

Just then Nina came into the room. She had put on makeup, but her pallor and the dark circles under her eyes showed through.

"Mrs. Sellars?" Deputy Switzer addressed her.

"Yes." Her voice was so faint we could hardly hear it.

"Your father tells me he just woke you up. How long have you been asleep?"

"It must have been three-thirty or four when I went upstairs. I went to sleep immediately and slept till they woke me a few minutes ago."

"When and where was the last time you saw Mr. Sellars?"

"I passed him in the kitchen when I went upstairs."

"I'm going to call the SBI to come and go over the scene for evidence before we remove the body. It's perfectly possible that this is a death by natural causes. But because of the circumstances, I'm going to treat it as suspicious until proven otherwise. It will take an autopsy to find that out; and that could take several days."

Frank was looking ill. "My daughter and I will stay here, of course. But would it be all right for Mrs. Poag here to go home? She hasn't been too well, and you can contact her in Greensboro if you need to."

"Yes. Just tell me how to reach you, Mrs. Poag, and you can leave now."

I looked at Frank questioningly. I felt as though I was abandoning them. But he was right. The day had taken a terrible toll on me.

"Here," Frank said pulling a set of keys out of his pocket, "take Nina's car. We have the rental one if we need it."

As I left, Frank had his arm around Nina, and she was crying softly.

Chapter
twenty-two

Before going to the motel, I stopped at a supermarket that was open all night and bought milk, orange juice, and a new two-liter bottle of Coke. I wasn't going to take a chance on the drinks in my refrigerator even though they were probably okay.

I slept soundly during the night. Whatever had knocked me out earlier was still probably lingering in my system. I would have slept even longer, but my natural alarm, Tee, stood over me on the bed demanding his morning meal. After thinking I might never see him again, I'll never again resent his morning "wake-up call." I gave him a big hug and kiss even though he squirmed, eager to get out of my grasp and down to the task of eating.

I lay there for a few minutes taking stock of myself and decided that I felt a great deal better than I had the night before. I wondered again what made me so sick. At least it seemed I wouldn't have any lasting effects from it.

After feeding Tee, I made myself a breakfast of cereal, fruit and coffee. I'd saved the old milk and juice in case they needed to be analyzed. While I ate at my dressing table, I thought about Frank and the last several days we'd spent together. I couldn't deny I was attracted to him. But I worried that I simply was flattered because he'd showed me some attention after this past lonely year. And I wondered, too, if my interest was enhanced by the fact we'd been thrown together in this crazy, adrenaline-raising situation. How would I feel about him in normal, humdrum circumstances? Maybe when this was all over, I'd have a chance to find out. But then he'd be going back to Wisconsin. So I'd better get a grip and not make a fool of myself.

My doctor's appointment wasn't till 9:30 and I was trying to think of something to do until then to keep my mind off of all that was going wrong for Nina. Delving into my purse for my lipstick, I came across the card that Ginger had given me with Alice Jeffries' name and number. It was pretty early to be calling someone, it was now 8 a.m., but I hoped I could catch her before she went out for the day.

To my surprise, she didn't even sound annoyed when I called her at that hour.

"I work at home," she told me when I asked if I could see her and explained the circumstances. "The film commission is based in Raleigh, but they have individuals spotted around the state who form sort of a network for them. Why don't you come on out around 8:30? I'll be glad to talk to you."

Alice, as I expected, lived in an upscale neighborhood, one of the newer ones that had been built on the north side of town around Lake Jeannette. Ginger had told me that her husband was an obstetrician-gynecologist which explained their ability to purchase a home in this pricey development. As interesting as her job must be bringing film-makers to our state, I didn't imagine that her salary was grand. Not working for the state government.

The Jeffries' house had all the peaks and angles and various roof lines that builders seem to relish anymore. I prefer simple, straightforward architecture myself. But there was little of that to be seen on the curving, wooded streets. It was if each builder tried to add one more jutting angle or a taller, more grandiose entryway than the one who built next door. I wondered how these homes would stand the test of time. Fifty years from now, would they be acclaimed as the quaint quintessential homes of the turn of the twenty-first century? Or would they be dismissed as misguided attempts at overdone opulence?

Alice's home was more subdued than most with its simple Georgian facade, but it was one of the largest on the street. She greeted me at the door in blue jeans,

Duke tee shirt and bare feet. She wore no makeup and had her light brown hair pulled back in a ponytail.

"Come in, come in," she said with a smile. "Why don't you come on back to the kitchen? I've got a pot of coffee on."

I followed her down a central hall and into a gorgeous kitchen that featured every new appliance known to man including a huge commercial stove. The pale wood cabinets that went on and on could have held nearly all my worldly goods, and the granite counter tops around the perimeter of the room and on the central island must have laid waste to a quarry. I wondered if the woman even cooked.

She led me to a table that fitted into a half circle of windows that looked out onto a stunning back yard filled with blooms in a rainbow of colors and well-tended shrubs and trees. A koi fish pond fed by an impressive waterfall that spilled over boulders was the centerpiece.

"Here, have a seat," she said, pulling out a chair the same pale beige as the cabinets. She poured two cups of coffee from a fancy looking coffee maker and set them on the table. "Cream or sugar?" she asked.

"No thanks."

She settled onto her chair and took a sip of her coffee. "Now, what is it I can do for you?"

"As I told you on the phone, I'm a friend of Nina's."

"Oh, yes. Nina Sellars. What a poor, misguided woman she is." She sighed and traced the rim of her cup with her finger.

"Meaning?" I asked.

"Well, the poor thing is so gullible. Anyone who would hook up with Cap Sellars deserves to have her head examined."

"So I have gathered from all that I've heard. You see, I only met Nina about three months ago when Cap was out west. I never did get to meet him. Can't say I've heard much good about him either. Nina may be naive or misguided, but she's as good hearted as they come. She was somehow blinded by her love for him. And she doesn't deserve to be accused of his murder. I can't conceive of her doing anything like that."

Alice leaned toward me and looked sober. "I agree with you. She's being railroaded. The circumstances under which he died are certainly strange though. I don't know the details, of course, but it sounds like they have a lot of evidence against her."

"That's true. And that's why I'm working so hard to find out what *really* happened. Ginger thought you might be able to tell me something that would be helpful."

She sighed and leaned back in the chair. "I don't know what. He'd been out of town for quite a while as you said. So I hadn't seen him recently except for the night he died. I did witness their argument."

"I understand that was over his insistence that he drive when he was drunk."

"Yes, Nina wouldn't give him the car keys. And I certainly didn't blame her. He was loaded."

"Did they often argue?"

"Not really. Not in public anyway. I know it hurt her when he flirted openly with other women, but if she fought about it, it was only in the privacy of their home. I think she felt insecure around our crowd, and she wouldn't have embarrassed herself and Cap by getting into an argument."

"So why that night?"

"She probably decided it was a matter of life and death. I sure wouldn't have gotten into a car with him in his condition. And maybe she was just kind of at the end of her rope with him. "

"Do you think she could have been so furious over his actions that night that she'd want to kill him?" I hoped she would give me an honest answer.

"No, absolutely not. It was especially sad for her that he died at that particular time."

"Why is that?"

She stood up. "Can I get you a refill? It takes about three cups before I'm fully awake."

"Sure," I said.

I waited a little impatiently while she poured more coffee in both our cups. Her statement had made me very curious.

"Cap and I would talk quite a bit at the parties. He quit hitting on me after I rejected his first attempt, but since I work with the film industry, we had a lot in common. He'd talk about his current projects, and one night, just before he left for California this last time, he even told me some personal stuff."

Now it sounded like we were getting somewhere. "I'm all ears."

"He admitted to me that he'd been having a hot and heavy affair, but he'd tired of it, and realized that Nina had always been there for him, through thick and thin, and he decided to try to make it up to her. I think he was a little ashamed of his behavior. And that was really something for a womanizer like Cap."

"Someone else told me they thought he'd decided to stay in his marriage."

"Yep. As I said, it is particularly tragic that he died just as things were getting better for them."

"Did he ever tell you who the mysterious Allison was?"

"No. That was the only time he ever got into their personal life, and I think he was feeling a lot of remorse. He apparently wanted to bury the past and get on with his life with Nina."

"Did he ever talk about his brother Daniel?"

"Why do you ask that?"

"He died last night. He was here from New York for the funeral."

"Oh my God! That's unreal! How did he die?"

"We don't know yet. It could have been natural causes or it could be suspicious. It'll depend on what the autopsy says."

"How perfectly awful for Nina."

Oh, yes, I thought, especially since it happened at her house. Another strike against her. "I just wondered if Cap ever mentioned Daniel. Did he say anything about how they got along?"

Alice stirred her coffee with a spoon even though she took it black. "I'm trying to think. I do believe he spoke of him once. It was when he told me about his affair. Said he and his brother used to see one another every time he went to New York. But he hadn't seen him since the affair started. That was another reason he was giving her up, so he could mend his relationship with his brother."

I thought how ironic it would be if Daniel *had* killed Cap just when Cap had decided to make up with him.

I drained my cup and stood up. "I'm sure you need to get to work, and I won't take any more of your time. I do appreciate your talking to me."

She rose to show me out. "I hope things get straightened out for Nina. She had enough grief from Cap. She doesn't deserve all this."

I had just enough time to get to the doctor's office. And, amazingly, I was put in the exam room almost immediately. This guy's got his act together, I thought, having often spent many an hour waiting for doctors.

When he came in the room, he carefully checked me over: taking my blood pressure, listening to my heart, looking down my throat and in my eyes.

"Looking good," he said, folding up his stethoscope into a bundle and sticking it in his pocket before starting to write notes on his clipboard. "You don't seem to have any ill effects."

"The question is ill effects of what?" I asked as I buttoned up the top two buttons of my blouse.

"I thought you knew." He looked up at me in surprise.

"How would I know?" Was he playing games with me? No one at the hospital had told me anything.

"You had a large amount of barbiturates in your system. I assumed you'd taken a handful of sleeping pills."

"Why would I do that?" I felt insulted. It was beginning to dawn on me that Dr. Kowicki thought I'd tried to kill myself. Couldn't he tell I wasn't the kind of person who would do such a thing? But I guess would-be suicides come in all shapes, sizes and ages.

He appeared somewhat taken aback by my question. "Did you not intend to...um...," He clearly wasn't comfortable, so I decided to help him out.

"Absolutely not. I have no idea how that happened."

"You're sure now. I can refer you to an excellent psychiatrist who can help..."

"You've got it all wrong. I wouldn't consider doing anything like that." Why wouldn't he believe me?

"We're going to have to report it to the police then." He was tapping his pen on the board, probably trying to decide whether to take my word for it or not.

"The only thing I can think of is that someone put something in my food. But I live alone and keep my door locked at all times. And I'm the only one who has a key. Remember the Tylenol incident years ago when someone tampered with a bottle? Do you think someone could have tampered with my food at the store or the warehouse?" I knew I was grasping at straws, but I was so scared it might be traced back to Nina's house. I couldn't let that happen. She had so many strikes against her already.

"Almost everything is packaged to prevent tampering these days," the doctor said. "I suppose it could be possible, but I'm sure there's some other explanation. At any rate, I'll contact the police."

I felt desperate now. The only way I could keep Nina out of this was to lie—once again. "I happen to have a good friend in CID," I said. "Why don't you let me take care of it. He'll give it individual attention, I'm sure."

The doctor looked dubious but he finally said, "All right, that would speed up the process. I'll let you take care of it then. He can contact my office for details." I knew that if he didn't hear from the police in a day or two, he would contact them. At least it would delay the inevitable. He handed me the clipboard with the charges to take to the cashier and said I didn't need to come back unless I had further problems.

When I got back to the motel, Frank had left a message so I called him back.

"Hi, Tommi. I finally got those telephone bills. I'll tell you, I think that computer's down more than it's ever running. Can I come to your place so we can go over them?"

"Of course. How's Nina?"

"She's still asleep. It was after two before the police and SBI cleared out last night. I told her before we went to bed that I might have to go to Greensboro on important business this morning."

"Are you sure you should leave her alone?" I asked.

"I took care of that too. I told her I was going to hire someone to do some housework for her since she hadn't felt up to it. Her former house cleaner had quit to have a baby just before Cap came home, and Nina hasn't had a chance to hire a replacement. What I'm really going to do is contact a woman I know. She's retired from the marines and can make the motions of cleaning house while really keeping an eye on her. Last I heard she was enjoying retirement and not tied down, so I'm pretty sure she'll be available."

"I'd feel much better knowing someone's there with her."

"I'll come as soon as I can get this squared away."

I took a leisurely shower. I wasn't quite ready to take a tub bath, afraid I'd relive the trauma of yesterday. Afterward I stood in front of my closet trying to decide what to wear. I hadn't taken this much interest in how I looked in a long time. I finally decided on a jade knit pantsuit with blue trim.

Frank got there a little after eleven.

"You must feel better," he said, putting a briefcase on a bed and sitting beside it. "You're looking great."

"Thanks. I think I might live." Though I indeed felt much improved, I'd also put color on my cheeks to look as healthy as possible.

"But you will see the doctor."

"I just got back from there. He says I'm doing very well." I decided not to tell Frank that he thought I'd tried to kill myself, or that I'd lied to him about contacting the police. I just didn't want to get into it with him." Did you reach your friend?"

"Yes. Luckily Diane was free and came on out to the house right after I talked to her. Nina was up by then and readily accepted her as domestic help. I think it will work out fine." He put the briefcase on his lap and opened it, pulling out a sheaf of bills. "These are the telephone bills. I haven't had a chance to look at them yet, because Nina got up right after I called Diane."

There were copies of the monthly bills for the past two years. Cap had used a post office box for his address in both California and Oak Ridge. It seemed obvious to me that he hadn't wanted Nina to get a look at them.

I sat beside Frank, looking over his shoulder as he scanned the pages. Cap had made many phone calls each month, and his charges ran several hundred dollars on each bill.

"Look at all these calls to New York," I pointed out. "Why don't I try calling some of them. If they're businesses, they'll answer with the firm's name. If no one answers, they're probably personal. So if we find a lot of calls to the same phone number, couldn't you find out who it's listed to?"

"Sure. The problem is he might have been contacting Allison at work."

"Oh, shoot, that's true. Why don't I ask for Allison each time I call?"

"It's worth trying."

I began dialing the New York numbers, jotting down the name of each company as I reached them and noting the response so I would not inadvertently call them again.

At the Kazmirof Theatrical Agency an Allison Mercer came to the phone.

"Cap Sellars wanted me to get in touch with you," I told her.

"Cap who?"

"Sellars."

"Never heard of him."

"He's a screenwriter; he's had business with your agency." It sounded fishy to me that she didn't even know his name, especially since it was connected with the industry.

"Well, I don't deal with those kind of people. They get the royal treatment from the big shots. I'm just a part-time secretary, and I never meet anyone who's even remotely important. I think you have the wrong person."

"Sorry," I said.

Frank had been watching me with anticipation. "Dead end?"

"Yeah. She didn't know him. I feel sure she was telling the truth."

No other businesses I called employed an Allison. Two of the numbers I dialed were not answered, making me think they were home phones.

"Let me call the office and find out who those two are. Too bad I don't have my laptop with me," Frank said. While he was doing that, I held Tee on my lap and stroked him. I missed my rocking chair. And Tee was missing the attention I usually gave him. He was acting exceptionally needy these days. If ever a "mew" sounded like a whine, he'd become the master of it.

It wasn't long before Frank had the information. One of the phone numbers belonged to a tailor shop and the other listing was for Daniel.

"Why don't we check out some of the California calls then?" Frank said. "Maybe Allison was out there all along."

I spent another half hour calling various locations in California. Even though most of them were around L.A. they each seemed to have a different area code. I came across one other Allison who worked at a specialty food store in Santa Monica. She vaguely remembered Cap's name and put me on hold while she checked their records.

"He occasionally orders a box of special stuffed dates that we order from the Near East. Was there a problem with the last shipment?"

"No, no. The telephone number got separated from the name of your store, and we were just trying to find out who the number belonged to. Thanks." I shrugged when I hung up. "Three strikes and we're out, Frank."

We had been through a whole year's worth of telephone bills and had come up empty.

"Let me look at the rest of the bills," I said. "Some of those would date back to when they were living in California, wouldn't they? Maybe something would show up in them."

When I got to the February bill from a year earlier, I found a number of calls to Reidsville.

"Frank, do you know Michelle's telephone number?"

He looked at me in surprise. "Michelle? Yes, it's 943-1582. Why?"

"Well, look. Her number appears a bunch of times on these bills. I was under the impression that Nina and Michelle were not close. Would Nina have called her that often?" I handed the papers to Frank.

"Strange," he said as he looked them over. "I've never known them to communicate much. And besides, these calls are from his business phone, not his home phone. But why would Cap call her?"

"I don't know. I was hoping you could tell me." My suspicions were beginning to grow, but I wasn't ready to share them with Frank at this point.

Frank handed the bills back to me. "There's probably some simple explanation. Why don't we talk to Michelle and find out what it's about."

"Look," I said, showing Frank an entry on another page, "here's a Greensboro number that appears pretty frequently too. Let me call it and see what it is."

I dialed the number. A voice at the other end said, "Belk's Department Store. Linen Department."

"Hold on a minute, please," I said putting my hand over the mouthpiece. "It's the linen department at Belk's. What should I do?" I whispered to Frank. Either Cap or Nina had called Michelle not only at home but also at work, and I doubted very much that it was Nina. Frank looked as if he'd been hit in the gut. "Ask for Michelle. Arrange to have lunch with her," he said.

After a brief conversation I hung up. "She called in sick today."

"Let's go out to her house then. I'm sure there's some simple explanation for this," Frank said. I knew he was in denial at this point even though it was evident something was going on between Cap and Michelle. It seemed like such an unlikely relationship, that I wanted to reject it too, but I couldn't.

"Before we do that, I'd like to stop off at Belk's and talk to her co-workers. Since so many calls were made to the store, someone there might talk about it more readily than Michelle would." What workplace doesn't revel in gossip?

"Is all this necessary?" Frank wasn't ready yet to accept the obvious. And I couldn't blame him.

"I think it's the best way," I answered. If it got to be too much for Frank, I'd go on by myself.

Frank drove the rental car, leaving Nina's car and my Mitsubishi at the motel. We'd decided to return the rental later in the day, and Frank would drive Nina's car back to Oak Ridge.

When we arrived at Friendly Shopping Center where Belk's was located, I asked Frank to wait in the car. "I think two of us would be too intimidating. Don't mean to be sexist, Frank, but in this case I think they might open up more readily to a woman."

He sighed and threw up his hands. "You're the boss."

I spontaneously gave him a peck on the cheek. "I kinda like that. I've not had much chance to be boss before."

The center was not crowded. Weekday mornings were always that way. I seldom shopped here but knew that at night or on weekends it could be a mob scene. It was one of only two major shopping centers in Greensboro.

Belk Department Store was located near Friendly Avenue for which the shopping center was named. I went in the front entrance, unsure of the location of the linen department. Racks and racks of women's clothes and a cosmetics counter occupied most of that level.

The directory near the escalator indicated that the linens were in the basement, so I rode the escalator down. I walked through the china and silver department where elegant table settings sparkled with lead-cut glassware, Bavarian china and fine silver. The linen department was back in the corner. Some of the price tags took my breath away. Lace-embellished down comforters with matching pillow shams and dust ruffles cost as much as a week's pay. But they were beautiful. I wondered how they would look with cat hair all over them. That made me chuckle a bit. And heavens knows I needed a laugh.

There was a counter with a cash register in the middle of the department where a tiny, wiry woman was talking on the phone. She had an astonishing amount of black hair piled on top of her head so that she looked as though she might topple over from the weight of it.

I waited quietly in front of the counter till the woman finished talking. It sounded like a personal call, and she seemed in no great rush to end it. I yearned to grab the phone out of her hand and say "Doggone it, woman, wait on me," but I managed to resist the temptation.

Finally she hung up. "May I help you?" she asked with little enthusiasm.

"Oh, I hope so," I said ingratiatingly. "This is kind of a personal thing, actually."

The woman looked at me with some distaste. "Oh?"

"You see, I'm Michelle Poag's cousin." Well, I almost was by my former marriage. "I'm real concerned about her." I was working hard to affect "down home" congeniality.

"How so?" Her attention level was definitely picking up now.

"She's had this relationship, you know what I mean? There's this guy who's been real interested in her. He calls her a lot, says he's crazy about her."

"Oh, you must mean Oscar."

Bingo! Not many people knew Cap's real name was Oscar. If Michelle wanted to hide his identity, she could call him that and no one would connect the two names.

"Right. That must be him. All of a sudden he stopped calling her." I hoped my expression looked like one of sincere concern.

"I know. Poor thing. She's really been in the dumps about it." It didn't take Miss Beehive long to get into the swing of sharing gossip.

That confirmed my hunch that when Cap died, Michelle, not wanting her co-workers to know who Oscar really was, pretended that he'd suddenly dumped her. I leaned across the counter and spoke in a low voice, taking the saleslady into my confidence. "She told me she was staying home sick today, but I think she's just sick about losing him. Who knows what she's going to do. I'm scared silly, you know? I want to help her, but I know almost nothing about him, and she won't talk about it. I was hoping maybe I could make her realize that he isn't worth all this. He must be a real jerk to do this to her. Can you tell me anything about this guy?"

"I wish I could help, but I only know his first name."

"How'd she meet him anyhow? See, I just moved back into town so I wasn't around when she was going with him. Now she just clams up on the subject."

Miss Beehive's face showed her delight in being able to participate vicariously in such a drama. She was eager to share everything she knew about Michelle's lover. "She went to New York City on vacation almost two years ago and met him there," she said, her eyes shiny with pleasure. "She knew his brother somehow and looked him up, and Oscar was there visiting from California. They saw each other every day that week and became lovers. After that when he had business in New York, he would pay for Michelle to fly up there over the weekend to meet him."

"Oh my gosh. That is *so* romantic. What do you think happened that caused him to drop her all of a sudden?"

"He kept telling her he was going to dump his wife and marry her. I told her it was the usual line that men dish out, but she really believed him. But about a week ago he stopped calling her. Just like that. And she had no idea why. Poor Michelle. It really broke her heart."

"Anything else you know that might help me snap her out of this?" I asked. I couldn't imagine what that could be. Cap not only decided to break it off with her, he up and died which made her chance of a reconciliation null and void.

"I don't think so," the saleslady said shaking her head. "I told her all along that married men are poison. They never leave their wives. I should know. I've fallen for two of them. Maybe Michelle should have gone for the brother instead. She said he wasn't married."

"Sounds like she chose the wrong one," I said. I wondered if Daniel had known about their affair. He'd always claimed he didn't know who Allison was. Had he helped her keep the secret? Or was he her lover first, before she got involved with Cap? Could my imagined scenario about him killing Cap out of jealousy have been for real?

Chapter
twenty-three

Frank was studying a state map he'd gotten from the glove compartment when I returned to the car.

"Taking a trip?" I asked. He probably wished he were.

"Just trying to pass the time. I'm the kind who reads cereal boxes at the breakfast table. How'd it go?"

I didn't know how to tell him what I'd learned without hurting him. But he'd find it out eventually. "It went well. Her co-worker reveled in telling all."

"And?"

I took his hand and held it, trying to soften the blow. "Michelle is really Allison."

Frank closed his eyes for a moment. "I was afraid of that. I kept hoping there was some innocent explanation for those phone calls, that maybe Cap wanted her advice on his marital problems. But I knew that was unlikely. How will I ever tell Nina? How could she do that to her own sister?"

"Since they never had a chance to become close, I suppose to Michelle it was no different than sleeping with anyone's husband. And that just doesn't bother some people. And, Frank, do we really need to tell Nina? What good would it do? It would only hurt her more."

We sat in silence for several minutes. Finally I said, "Forgive me for saying this, but I can't understand what the attraction was. Nina is the more attractive of the two. Michelle seems so...well...a little on the crude side."

"I think it's all coming together for me now. I'd noticed that too. That isn't the normal Michelle. She hasn't looked or acted like herself since I've been here, and I couldn't figure out what had gotten into her. But now it seems obvious. She wanted to throw anyone off the scent who might even suspect her of being this Allison person. No stranger would guess Cap was interested in anyone so unattractive. When she's fixed herself up, Michelle can be quite pretty. Of course, it could be that she gave up trying to look nice when Cap decided to stay in his marriage. She probably thought what's the point? And she normally isn't so...crude, as you called it. No one in the family would ever have suspected her of having an affair with her own brother-in-law."

"Shall we go talk to her then?" I put it as a question so that if Frank was squeamish about it, I could take him back to the motel.

"I dread it, but yes."

We spoke very little on our way to Reidsville. The air was cooler and less humid, and if it had been a normal day, we would have delighted in its crisp, invigorating breezes. I noticed that the leaves on the tulip poplars had begun to fall. After a dry summer they would often just curl up and turn brown, dropping off abruptly. It would appear as if the tree were dying, but it always budded again in the spring. I thought of Frank and how his optimism must be dying in him right now, succumbing to the onslaught of evidence against his daughters. But he was strong. Like the tree, he'd recover after time, as he had recovered from his wife's death.

Finally we arrived at Michelle's house, pulling into the driveway behind her Suburban. Both of us sat in the car for a few minutes, dreading the encounter that was to come. But I knew we might as well face it and get it over with. I stepped out of the car and went to the front door, Frank following reluctantly behind.

The door was open and I peered into the living room, but it was empty. I rapped hard upon the screen door. After a couple of minutes, Michelle appeared from the bedroom side of the house, dressed in a wildly flowered housecoat. Her hair was uncombed and she had no makeup on. Maybe she was attractive when she was dressed up, as Frank had claimed, but no one would know it to see her now. She looked like the wrath of God.

"What on earth are you two doing here?" she said when she saw us.

Frank came up behind me and said, "We heard that you were sick and came to see how you are."

Michelle felt her forehead as though checking for a fever. "I think I've got some kind of bug or something. But, come in if you're not afraid of catching it." She unlocked the screen door and held it open, inviting us inside with a lackluster wave of the hand.

"Thanks," I said. "We'll try not to get too close."

Frank and I sat on the sofa while Michelle dropped into a chair as though she could scarcely stand. "How did you know I was sick?" she asked.

"We wanted to have lunch with you," I said, "but when we called you at work they told us you were home today."

"Oh." Michelle laid her head back on the chair and closed her eyes. I wondered if she felt that bad or if she was a consummate actress, a skill Michelle must possess from the way she had deceived me with her coarseness.

Finally Michelle straightened up and said, "Was there something you wanted to talk about? Was that why you called me for lunch?"

I thought I'd better do the talking, to spare Frank as much as possible. "Yes, there is, Michelle. We got a copy of Cap's phone records for the past couple of years." I watched Michelle's face closely for some sign of emotion, but there was none. "There were a lot of calls to Reidsville and even to Belk's."

Michelle stared at me with a stony expression. So I continued.

"I just talked with your co-worker at the department store, the one with the beehive hairdo. She says you've been having a passionate affair with someone named Oscar."

Michelle glared at me now, loathing in her eyes. "So what?"

"Cap's name happens to be Oscar. Miss Beehive also told me you met him in New York City through his brother. Doesn't that rather narrow it down?" How long was she going to stonewall us? It was making it more difficult for Frank if she was going to play games.

Michelle stood up and walked over to the living room window, staring out into the yard, her arms crossed defiantly over her chest. Once she started talking, it was if she couldn't stop. It came pouring out. "Okay, so I was in love with Cap. He was the greatest thing that ever happened to me. I'd contacted Daniel when I went to New York because I thought maybe he could get me some theater tickets or could recommend restaurants. Cap happened to be in town on business, and Daniel invited both of us over for dinner at his apartment. Since Nina got married in California, I'd never met him. I always thought love at first sight was something the romance writers dreamed up, but it really happened to me. I was crazy about him, and he said he'd fallen for me too. But we kept it secret from Daniel because we didn't want it to get back to Nina."

Frank finally spoke in a stricken voice. "How could you do that to your sister, Michelle?"

She whirled around to face her father with fury in her eyes. "What the hell do I owe her? She's never done anything for me. She led this highfalutin' life while I've always had to struggle for everything. I decided that it was my turn now!"

"But," I interjected, "he was thinking of ending the affair and staying with Nina, wasn't he?"

"No!" Michelle shouted. "That's not true." She just couldn't bring herself to admit that he'd lost interest in her.

"That's what Miss Beehive told me," I said. "And it came directly from you, she said."

"I only told her that to explain why he hadn't called me this past week. I couldn't keep up the pretense of being happy after Cap died, so I told her I was depressed because he'd dumped me. That was the only way of explaining the end of our relationship without confessing who he really was and that he'd died." She sounded so sincere I would have believed her, except for the fact that Alice had confirmed he was going back to Nina. Ernie Zaleski had said so too.

"Don't you have some idea who killed him then?" I asked. "Maybe he told you things he didn't tell anyone else."

Michelle flopped down in the chair again with a frown. She looked at her father a while before she spoke. "I think that Nina really did do it. She didn't want to lose him. But even more than that, she didn't want to lose his money. He'd told me how worried he was she might do something terrible."

Frank sat forward on the sofa, his face reflecting such pain and grief as I had never seen before. "Michelle, how could you believe that about your own sister?"

"Look, Dad, part of the reason I hadn't admitted the truth about Cap and me was because I thought my testimony would be very damaging to Nina if I were put on the witness stand. So I've kept my mouth shut. At least give me credit for that."

Frank buried his face in his hands. I wanted to hold and comfort him, but I would not do it in front of Michelle.

So I changed the subject. "Look, Michelle, did you have any boyfriends about the time you met Cap? I mean could there be someone out of his mind with jealousy, who might have wanted him dead?"

Michelle shook her head. "The last guy I dated before I met Cap dumped me, not vice versa. In fact the jerk decided to go back to the wife he'd been separated from for a year. I'd vowed I was going to be celibate I was so fed up with men. But then I met Cap, and my vow went out the window. Maybe it's a cliché, but he was the love of my life." A tear rolled down her cheek as she said it. She might have been a great teller of lies, but I had to believe her when she said she loved Cap.

"Did you know Daniel is dead?" I asked her.

"I saw that in the morning paper." She seemed unmoved by this fact. Her tears were for Cap alone.

"Have you an explanation for that too?" I asked.

"What's that snide remark supposed to mean?" Michelle's voice was strident.

"I'm not being snide. I just wanted your thoughts on it." I probably should have let up on her, but there were too many loose threads, and I wanted answers.

"It was probably an accidental overdose. Cap said he took a lot of uppers and downers, and this time he must have taken too many. Probably mixed them with liquor."

"Did you know I ate or drank something that sent me to the hospital?" I asked her.

Michelle looked shocked. "No!"

"I thought maybe it was connected to Daniel's death in some way."

"I don't know. I can't imagine how."

"Well," I stood up, "I guess that about covers it. If only we'd known you were Allison sooner, it would have saved us a lot of time and effort."

"I'm sorry you found out," Michelle said looking at her father, her face reflecting both regret and intractability. "I didn't want Dad to know."

Michelle and Frank got up simultaneously. He went over to hug her. "Sorry, Babe, if I came on like Attila the Hun. I'll try to be more understanding. But it really tears me apart when my children hurt each other."

She held him off at arm's length. "You don't want my germs," she said stiffly.

"Okay, Michelle," he said sadly.

It looked like a permanent chasm was opening up between father and daughter. I think he was trying hard to forgive her, but she was unrepentant.

We left the house as Michelle returned to her bed.

Chapter
twenty-four

Once seated in the car, Frank crossed his arms over the top of the steering wheel and wearily lowered his head to them. He was bereft.

I touched his shoulder. "I'm truly sorry, Frank." I wanted to say more but didn't know how to put it into words. How do you comfort a friend when his own daughter whom he loved and trusted has betrayed that trust? I knew that there was little anyone else could do to lessen the hurt.

For a few minutes he didn't move or speak. Finally, he raised his head and turned on the motor. "I don't know which is worse. To learn that Michelle was Cap's lover or to hear her accuse her sister of his murder." His voice had a catch in it. Frank, unlike Bernard, had no fear of letting his emotions show.

"That's purely speculation, the part about Nina. Jealousy can do terrible things to people's minds. Their imaginations really get out of control."

He nodded mutely. "Where now?"

Suddenly it was important to me to visit the scene of the crime. "We need a break. Let's get a carry-out lunch and go over to Lake Brandt."

"Lake Brandt? Why there? I thought you wanted a break from the case." Frank looked at me with genuine puzzlement.

"Oh, come on, Frank. It's one of the prettiest places in town, and it's on the north side of town barely out of our way home. It's too pretty today to eat inside some stuffy restaurant."

Frank said nothing. It was obvious he didn't want to go there, but all the fight had been knocked out of him. I hated to see him withdraw this way, hoping that facing the scene of the crime might induce him to again become the forceful person he'd been the night he arrived in town. Of course, I was taking a chance that it might be the moment that would throw him into total despair.

On the way back to Greensboro I worked hard at keeping a conversation going, talking about things unrelated to the case. I made sure we stayed in neutral territory; we both were pretty emotionally fragile at this point. Frank at first had little to say, but slowly relaxed and became gradually more talkative. He even smiled once or twice.

He pulled into a Wendy's drive-through line on Battleground, and we both ordered cheeseburgers, fries, and Cokes and laughed as the bag was passed to us.

"Talk about criminal action," I said as I peeked in the bag and pulled out a couple of french fries to nibble on. "Is there a law against consuming this many calories?"

We drove into Lake Brandt park through heavily wooded and gently rolling terrain, especially beautiful today with its lake reflecting the beginnings of autumn color in the surrounding trees. The serenity of the scene touched us immediately. Frank pulled into the parking lot, and we carried our lunch to one of the picnic tables that afforded an unsurpassed view of the lake. We were close to the infamous boat ramp. Since it was a weekday and shortly after two o'clock few people were around. A young woman was eating lunch with a toddler on the other side of the picnic area, and there were a few small boats with fishermen out in the center of the lake.

"I love this place most in the fall," I said. "The maples and sweet gum around the edge of the lake are twice as beautiful when they're reflected in the water." I swung my legs up onto the bench and stretched my head back, working out the kinks in my neck. "I don't know why I love fall so much since it reminds me of middle age. You know darn well that winter is coming. I should prefer spring with all the newness. But you know, sometimes I think middle age has its good points.

At least you've kind of figured life out. You know it's neither as good nor as bad as you once imagined it to be."

Frank nodded absently while nibbling on a fry. I noticed he had yet to unwrap his sandwich. Apparently he had little appetite.

"You come to accept it as it is," I continued, "and try to make the most of it. Hopefully."

"I used to agree with that," Frank said, "but I'm beginning to think it's worse than I ever imagined."

I could feel my face grow warm. Why on earth was I pontificating like some New Age guru when Frank was dealing with devastating news from all sides? I could be such a jackass sometimes.

I picked up my Coke and took a long drag on the straw. I was too embarrassed to say anything more.

Frank unwrapped his sandwich, but did nothing but pick tiny pieces off the bun and throw them to the ducks who came quacking officiously around the table.

After I finished my lunch, I took off my shoes and socks and rolled up the legs of my slacks.

"What's up?" Frank asked, still tossing bits of bun. The hamburger lay on the square of wrapper looking like road kill.

"It's so pretty. I'm going to wade a bit. Would you like to join me?"

"Think I'll just wait here and spoil the ducks. I have very tender feet," he almost smiled. "I wouldn't get from here to that tree." He pointed to a tree about fifteen feet away.

"Okay. I'll be right back."

I walked down to the lake and peered into the water. Recent rains had made it muddy, a condition that was more common in the spring. But early September had brought several thunderstorms after a very dry summer, and the water level was high.

I went over to the boat ramp and walked slowly along the edge of the water across the ramp, carefully planting one foot in front of the other, hoping to find something. Then I turned around and came back, only a little farther out on the concrete which sloped slowly at first and then dropped off rapidly. I continued my walk back and forth until just before the drop off point. I was beginning to lose hope that my hunch was correct, when I felt something under my foot. I leaned over and picked it up. It was a squarish wire thing, several inches in diameter, with wires in parallel rows across it. I shook the water off it and ambled slowly back toward the picnic table where Frank sat, not at all anxious to face the next few minutes.

"What have you got there?" he asked as I laid it on the table in front of him.

"What I was looking for," I said, hating that I'd found it, yet elated at the same time.

"Would you mind explaining that?" His voice was soft, his look cautious.

I climbed over the bench and sat down to face him. "I'm sorry I didn't say anything, Frank. But there was no point in mentioning it unless I actually found it."

His look turned to alarm now. "What on earth are you talking about?"

"When we came out of Michelle's house, I walked in front of her Suburban to get to the passenger side of your car. I noticed that she had one of these headlight protectors on the left side, but none on the right side. She probably never noticed it was missing."

Frank picked it up and turned it over and over examining it. "You think this came from Michelle's Suburban?"

"I'd be willing to bet a mint on it." They really weren't that common; I'd only seen a few. It wasn't standard equipment, but something the owner would have to add to the car.

"You're saying then…" He couldn't finish the sentence.

"I'm saying that I think it was Michelle who pushed Cap's car into the lake."

Frank couldn't seem to find any words at first. It was another terrible blow he'd have to absorb. Finally he said, "But why? You said yourself that his mistress had nothing to gain and everything to lose by his death."

"But that was when I thought everything was okay between them. Then—remember?—Ernie Zaleski told you he thought maybe Cap had decided to stay with Nina. And I talked to one of their friends who said he'd confided the same thing to her. He'd decided to give up his affair and try to make his marriage work. Some people do commit murder when they are rejected."

How I hated this. I'd just gotten Frank to smile again, if only just barely, to put aside his problems for even a few minutes. Now I was having to tell him things that would devastate any father.

"Dear God in heaven," he said. "I couldn't believe Nina was capable of murder, and now you're saying that Michelle did it? How could I have raised a child like that?" he groaned.

"Oh, Frank, don't ever blame yourself. Parents can do their very best, but kids don't always turn out the way they want them to. All kinds of things happen to them in the real world that can undo all they taught them. People could go crazy if they had to accept responsibility for everything their adult offspring do."

Frank dropped the headlight protector on the table as though it were on fire. "What do we do now?"

"I think we should go back to Reidsville, confront Michelle, and try to talk her into giving herself up. She might be able to plead temporary insanity."

Frank wiped tears from his eyes with the back of his hand. "I want to tell her to run, to leave the country, but I couldn't do that to Nina. Why does it have to be one or the other of my children?" He seemed to be asking the heavens rather than me. Finally he pulled the car keys from his pocket and handed them to me.

Wordlessly we walked to the car, and I got in on the driver's side. I drove out of the park and headed back toward Reidsville.

Chapter
twenty-five

We barely spoke on the way to Michelle's. I knew I could not distract Frank even temporarily from what probably awaited us. Did he resent the fact I found the headlight protector? Although it almost certainly was indicative of Michelle's guilt, at the same time it could prove Nina's innocence. I couldn't vindicate them both, much as I wished I could.

When we arrived at Michelle's house, we both walked around to the front of the Suburban. I pulled the wire protector from my purse and held it up beside the one on the left headlight. It was a perfect match. Though I didn't say so to Frank, I doubted that this evidence alone would be enough to convict Michelle. We had to force the issue now—I knew she had to confess. Knowing Michelle, that wasn't going to be easy to accomplish. I felt less than optimistic.

I slipped the wire gadget back into my purse and went up to the front door followed by Frank, who still had said nothing. He looked as world weary and despondent as someone who'd lost a loved one. In a way he had.

After I knocked on the screen door, Michelle again appeared from the bedroom area. Instead of opening the door for us, she crossed her arms and looked at us sulkily. "Look, I'm sick. Why don't you two leave me alone?"

Frank moved me gently aside and faced Michelle squarely. "We must talk to you. Now!"

Looking very glum, she opened the door and stepped back so we could enter the room. She didn't invite us to sit, but we both sat down on the sofa. I didn't know whether I was going to have to tell her why we were there, or Frank would do it. I decided to take the burden from him.

Michelle stood in the middle of the room, hands thrust in her pockets, looking at us with defiance. "So, say whatever you have to say so I can get back to bed. I've already told you everything I know about Cap. What more is there?"

I stood up so I would be on Michelle's level. I reached into my purse and pulled out the wire protector. "*This* is what's more."

Michelle stared at it unsuspectingly, but I could see the recognition growing in her eyes and could sense her struggle to conceal her alarm. "What's that?" she said making a disparaging gesture toward it.

"The headlight protector from the right headlight on your Suburban."

"So? Big deal." Michelle gave an exaggerated shrug. So she was going to stonewall me.

"It is a big deal since I found it under water at the boat ramp in Lake Brandt."

A flicker of fear crossed Michelle's face. "How do I know you didn't take it off the Suburban just now?"

"Because your father saw me pick it up at the lake. And he'll testify to that." I couldn't see Frank's expression since I was facing away from him and I didn't want to break eye contact with Michelle. But I knew he must be suffering as deeply as he'd ever suffered in his life. I hated this—to hurt him this way—but I had to do it.

Michelle glanced over to her father. From her expression, I knew he must have nodded in agreement.

I took a step toward Michelle who in turn fell back a step. "Look, Michelle," I said, "you already admitted that Cap was your lover. Now, if you'll admit that you were the one who pushed their car into the lake it'll go better for you. Don't make us turn you in. You need to give yourself up."

Michelle said nothing. Her expression became stony, recalcitrant. I realized that she was not going to give an inch.

Unexpectedly Frank jumped to his feet and stood beside me. I thought he'd be so emotionally overwrought that he would sit on the sidelines and let me do all the talking.

"How could you let your sister take the blame?" It came out in a cross between a roar and a cry of pain.

Michelle's eyes opened wide, and fury drove out the fear in them. She grabbed the headlight protector from me and threw it on the floor in disgust. "Why would you care so much?" she yelled. "Nina probably isn't your daughter anyway!"

Frank looked as if someone had slapped his face. He grabbed Michelle's arm. "How do you know that?"

Michelle's face softened as sadness replaced the anger. "Mom told me just before she died. While I was staying with her." Then her eyes narrowed and she shook off her father's hand in renewed resentment. "You know, one of those many, many weekends I spent with her when she was sick. Was Nina ever there? No!"

"Nina was in California then," Frank said weakly.

"She could have afforded to come back."

"She did twice." Frank sounded apologetic.

"Once to see Mom for two days and once for the funeral. I mean, let's face it, we wouldn't want to interfere with her social life, would we?" The sarcasm was thick and ugly.

"I don't think Cap wanted her to leave. He was always pretty controlling you know."

"Oh, brother! What a lame excuse," Michelle exclaimed. "Well, anyway, at least I found out why you and Bernard don't speak."

I stared at Frank. "Why, Frank? Tell me why!"

For a moment Frank shut his eyes, so overcome with anguish he couldn't talk. Finally he found his voice, but he spoke with great reluctance. "Marilyn and I had a terrible fight shortly before our wedding day. It was one of those ridiculous things that got all out of proportion, probably just nerves. A day or so later I learned she'd slept with Bernard. The son of a bitch seduced her when she was the most vulnerable. I told her I never wanted to see her again, but she begged for my forgiveness. She said she'd been so devastated by our breakup that she had lost her head. Bernard had taken advantage of her in a weak moment, and she was nearly suicidal when I found out."

He took a deep breath as if he were suffering physical pain. "We loved each other so much and had hurt each other almost beyond fixing. But I couldn't face losing her, so we eloped soon afterward." He stopped for a minute, unable to continue. Finally he shuddered and began again. "She got pregnant with Nina right away and...we never... we never knew who the father was. Marilyn insisted it was me, but I could never accept that. All these years I've never been sure I was Nina's father."

"Oh, Frank." I felt nauseated. Had I known this years ago would I have married Bernard? I very much doubt it. This would have happened shortly before I met him - a precursor of what he eventually did to me. He may have been having affairs throughout our marriage, but I was too naive to be aware of it.

"So why not let her take the blame? You *know* I'm your daughter, so you owe me," Michelle told her father. She was pleading now.

"Because she didn't do it." Frank looked at her with dismay. "Can't you understand that?"

Michelle was less defiant now, realizing finally that she really was in trouble. She sank down in a chair in a slouch that hinted of acquiescence. "It's too bad she didn't die. She was the one who was supposed to."

"What?" I had never expected this.

"What do you mean?" Frank shouted.

She waved us to be seated. "Sit down. I might as well tell you the whole thing."

We both sat back down on the sofa, taut with apprehension.

"Cap moved Nina back here because he thought it'd be easier to get a divorce here. Or at least he'd come out of it better. He was trying to appease her, too, so he'd have time to put most of his assets in the Caymans. And he was good hearted enough to have her back in North Carolina where she wanted to be when he left her."

"Like Ernie told you," I said to Frank.

"Something happened, though, and it was like he was falling in love with her all over again. Maybe it was the change of scenery. I don't know what. He hadn't come right out and told me he wasn't going to leave her, but I could tell what he was thinking. I was so sick and tired of Nina having everything and me nothing. I thought at last it was going to be my turn, but now even that one chance was going down the drain.

"Last Wednesday I'd gone to Greensboro to see a movie. On the way home I pulled up behind someone at a stoplight and was surprised to see it was Nina driving Cap's car. I thought she was alone. Cap must have been so drunk he was all slumped down in the seat and his head didn't show above the headrest.

"I decided to follow her. I thought she might be having an affair, and I could find out who it was and tell Cap. I was desperate to find anything I could use to turn him against her. When she drove into Lake Brandt Park, I turned off my headlights and went in behind her. I still had no plan. But when she stopped on that boat ramp, something just clicked in my mind. I knew I had to push her into the lake, and then I could have Cap all to myself."

Michelle looked down and picked at a stain on the front of her housecoat. Tears began to stream out of her eyes. "So what did I do but kill him instead?" She began to sob now.

Frank and I were too stunned to speak. All along we had assumed that Cap was the murderer's target.

I wished fervently I had a hidden mike. But if Michelle was confessing to us, I thought she must be planning to confess to the police as well.

"What about Colin, the kid?" I asked. "You must have put him up to the story about being at the lake."

Michelle shrugged tearfully. "Oh, sure. I've bought coke from Colin, so when I realized I needed an eyewitness to make it look like Nina did it, I told him I'd turn his name in to the cops on the Crimestoppers line if he didn't help me. The police could've set up a sting operation to catch him. He made the threatening phone calls too." She wiped her eyes and gave her father an accusing look. "I always knew you loved Nina more than you did me."

Frank obviously could barely endure another revelation from his daughter. "Of course I don't. What makes you say that?"

"You talked about her all the time." She pitched her voice lower to mimic his and rocked her head from side to side in an exaggerated imitation of a braggart. "Their house is so wonderful! Her husband is so talented! They have such a marvelous social life! Blah, blah, blah, ad nauseam." Her voice resumed its normal tone. "I hated hearing about her. I was sick of it all."

"Oh, Michelle," Frank said, "I had no idea I sounded that way to you. I was proud of what they'd accomplished, but no prouder of them than I was of the rest of my children. I thought you'd be interested in what they were doing. I never realized you resented it so much."

"So you stole her husband away to get back at her," I said. Sibling rivalry and jealousy can be one of the ugliest of all human conditions.

Michelle sat forward in the chair and looked at me with great seriousness. "Not so. I fell in love with Cap and he with me because we were attracted to each other, period. He could have been anybody. It was a fluke he was Nina's husband." She paused to give her next statement particular emphasis. "He told me I was much better in bed than Nina." She looked at her father, anticipating his response the way a naughty child displays a deliberately soiled diaper to its mother.

I could sense Frank's struggle to keep from reacting. For the next couple of minutes there was nothing but silence, broken only by the sound of a neighbor mowing.

Finally Michelle spoke. She leaned back into the chair and said, "Well, that's it. That's the story."

"Oh, no," I said. "Not by a long shot."

"What do you mean?" Michelle was on guard again.

"I want to know about that fire in my place. You had something to do with it, didn't you? I know my cat didn't start it." Who else but Michelle would have been motivated to hurt or kill me?

A slow smile spread across Michelle's face. I couldn't believe my eyes. Michelle was enjoying this. "Pushing the car into the lake was a spur-of-the-moment thing. I hadn't planned it at all. But the fire was something else." She smoothed down her housecoat and maintained her Cheshire Cat smile. "That was pretty ingenious, if I do say so myself."

It seemed to me that Michelle had passed over some invisible line. Up till now she had displayed normal fear and reticence in relating the events that night at Lake Brandt. But now it was as if her mind had slipped into an aberrant state, psychotic even. She was relishing the moment.

I decided I must play along with her. "It certainly was. The firemen never suspected foul play. You were very clever. How did you do it?"

"When I realized you were trying to free Nina, I decided I'd have to get rid of you. So after you came out to my house that first time, I went over to your place when you were gone. It was a snap to get in your sliding door by picking the lock. But I realized that when you were home, especially at night, you'd put the steel rod in the door track. When I found that your circuit breaker box was in the outside storage room, that made it real simple. I went back on Sunday afternoon and replaced the batteries in the smoke alarm with dead ones, flipped off the circuit breaker switch for the laundry room only and put the iron on top of a pile of clothes with the dial turned on."

If I hadn't been totally aware of the devious workings of her mind prior to this, I was now sure she was capable of almost anything.

"That night I came back, waited till I was sure you'd be asleep, and then flipped the circuit breaker switch back on. Didn't have to go in the house at all." By now she was smiling broadly, proud of her scheme. "I wanted it to look like an accident because I didn't want the police to get involved. Then they might make some connection to Cap's death. Didn't want to get them even thinking about it."

I glanced at Frank and saw the horror in his eyes.

"Michelle," he said, "you're talking about trying to kill Tommi."

"Yeah," she answered, the smile gone, "too bad it didn't work. If it had, you wouldn't be here talking to me, and Nina could spend the rest of her life in jail. Bum luck, that's what I always have."

I was feeling sick. More than anything, I wanted to leave, to get away from Michelle, but I wasn't finished yet.

"Daniel?" I threw out his name like a fisherman tossing out his line into the water.

Michelle closed her eyes. "Oh, yes, poor, poor Daniel. He was a nice guy."

"Did you have something to do with his death?" Frank asked. I was surprised he was able to say anything.

"Yeah," Michelle acknowledged, nodding her head vacantly. "He really didn't know about us, but I was afraid that since he'd introduced us, he might put two and two together. Or find something around Nina's house that might give it away. Couldn't take the chance."

"So you put something in his drink and my drink too."

"Barbiturates. Nina had them all over the house. She must have been into them pretty heavy before all of this happened. I just helped myself to them when I was over there."

"I can't figure out how you gave them to me."

"I went right over to your motel the day we had lunch together. You'd told me you had an appointment, so I knew you weren't going back there. All I had to do was wait outside your room till the maid went in to clean. They always leave the door open. When she went in to clean the bathroom, I snuck in and put it in your Coke bottle. You know, I thought sure the second time I tried to get rid of you would work like a charm, 'cept Dad here had to find you. You've got more lives than your damn cat. Which reminds me. You should have seen how friendly he was, rubbing up against me. I thought about putting something in his water dish, but he was too sweet to die." Michelle was getting more and more expansive. She was finally getting the attention she so craved.

"And what about Daniel?" I asked. This was a nightmare pure and simple.

"That was really a cinch. When you two were at the hospital yesterday, I called Daniel and asked if I could see him, told him I had something to tell him about Nina, but didn't want her to know we were meeting. He said she was asleep and wouldn't even know I was there.

"So I went over to her house and first thing asked him if he wanted a beer. Daniel never turns down a beer. I found that out in New York. I doctored his in the kitchen and drank along with him so he wouldn't be suspicious. Then I made up some cockamamie story about Nina telling me a month ago she wanted to kill Cap and asked him what I should do about it. He said he didn't believe me for a minute. He knew Nina better than that. Why was I accusing her? So I pretended to be mad at him and left. Apparently he dropped dead not long afterward." She said it almost flippantly.

"But you didn't harm Nina," I said, wondering why that was so when her original intention at Lake Brandt was to kill her sister.

"I figured she go to jail for both Cap's and Daniel's death. Maybe even go to Death Row. I liked that idea."

Frank stood up, walked over to his daughter's side and stooped down beside her chair. He picked up her hand and held it in both of his. "Michelle, maybe it's my fault what's happened to you. I've always loved you, and I thought you knew it. If I didn't make that clear, then all I can say is I'm very, very sorry." He stopped and bent his head down trying to regain control. "Why don't you go get dressed now. Tommi and I will take you back to Greensboro and you can tell your story to the police."

Michelle started crying again. "Do I have to, Daddy?"

"I don't think they'll put you in jail, Michelle, I think they'll send you to a hospital where you can get help. You want to get well, don't you?"

She nodded her head without saying a word and got up slowly and walked back toward the bedroom.

Frank returned to the sofa and sat beside me. "What in God's name have I done to my child?" he asked. It broke my heart.

I put my arms around him and drew him close. "Michelle's very, very sick. I don't believe you had anything at all to do with it. I'd bet the drugs she got from Colin are the culprit, or at least partially responsible."

"I wanted so desperately to have Nina cleared. I never dreamed it would mean losing another daughter."

"I know, I know."

I thought about the upcoming drive back to town as we waited for Michelle. I knew it would be dreadful. How would Michelle react? Would she change her mind about confessing? Would we be forced to turn her in against her will? If only we didn't have so far to go. But neither of us could bring ourselves to call the police to come to the house. At least she could retain a modicum of dignity by turning herself in.

I wondered what my relationship with Frank would be like when this ordeal was over. He'd never be able to forget that I was the one who exposed his daughter. And now the long-held secret about him and Bernard had been revealed, too. It was Bernard who should feel shame, not Frank. But I believed that men had an especially difficult time handling betrayal, as if it made them culpable. Why couldn't Frank write it off as Marilyn's weakness and Bernard's lechery? He was guilty of nothing. In fact, he had distinguished himself in his forgiveness of Marilyn. It was too much to ask him to forgive Bernard too.

No wonder Bernard was so anxious to handle Nina's case. She could be his daughter. I surprised myself by feeling a tiny amount of sympathy for him. After all, for most of her life, Nina had been inaccessible to Bernard. How difficult it must have been for him not knowing whose daughter she was and not being able to get to know her as she grew up. And of course Nina must not have an inkling about any of this. What an incredible mess it was.

"Hurry up, Michelle," Frank finally shouted in frustration. I knew that he wanted to get this over and done with before we all lost the will to proceed with it.

Michelle did not answer.

Frank stood up and began to pace. "I suppose she's getting all dressed up to go to the police station. Why doesn't she just throw on slacks and a shirt?"

"Why don't I see what's holding her up?" I said. I walked down the hall toward the bedrooms. One bedroom had a single bed all made up, the other a double bed with rumpled sheets and the spread thrown back. The light was on and an open book was on the night stand. The closet door was open, exposing a jumble of clothes, but the room was empty. Just down the hall the bathroom door was closed. I put my ear up to it to ascertain if Michelle was taking a shower. No water was running, but I thought I heard a low moan.

I tried the doorknob, but it was locked. I knocked on the door. "Michelle?" There was no answer.

I ran back to the living room. "Frank, I think there's something wrong with

Michelle. She's in the bathroom and the door's locked, but she won't answer me."

He jumped off the couch and sprinted down the hall, stopping before the bathroom and pounding on the door. "Michelle?" he called loudly. But there was only silence in response. He backed up against the hall wall and then threw his shoulder against the door with all his force. The door slammed open, and Frank stumbled into the room, unable to stop his momentum. He caught himself by grabbing the edge of the bathtub. "Oh, no!" he cried.

I was right behind him. There, stretched out in the tub was Michelle, her arms crossed over her chest, blood staining the front of her housecoat and streaks of it on the sides of the tub. Her wrists had been cut, wide and deep, and blood oozed out of them, pooling now beneath the wounds. A bloody razor was on the floor.

I jerked two hand towels from a towel bar and knelt down beside Frank, grabbing Michelle's closest arm and wrapping one tightly around her wrist to staunch the flow. Michelle resisted weakly but seemed to be in shock.

"I'll go call an ambulance," Frank said as he ran out of the room. As I wrapped the second towel around Michelle's other wrist, Frank reappeared. "They're on their way."

I was occupied with holding the towels as tightly on the wounds as possible. "She's in shock, Frank. Get a blanket to put over her."

He brought the spread from Michelle's bed and covered her with it, gently lifting her arms to tuck it around her as though he were tucking in a small child for the night. We both stayed beside her waiting for help to arrive, I applying pressure to the wounds, and Frank smoothing his daughter's hair, saying words of encouragement. After about ten minutes, the emergency crew arrived and took over, wrapping her wrists, checking her blood pressure. When they were sure Michelle was stable, they laid her on a stretcher and carried her to the emergency van for the trip to the hospital in Greensboro. We'd asked that they take her to

Wesley Long instead of Cone so we could be close to her. Frank and I followed in our car.

Chapter
twenty-six

Michelle's wounds turned out to look worse than they actually were. "Not too many people succeed in killing themselves that way," the doctor told us, "unless they go unattended for a very long time and lose a lot of blood. But wrist cuts generally aren't severe enough. She'll be fine." Physically maybe, but surely not mentally.

Frank wanted to stay with Michelle even though the hospital kept a close watch over her. He was consumed with guilt over all she had done.

"Why don't I go see Bernard and fill him in on everything," I suggested, knowing Frank would just as soon avoid meeting with him.

"Good idea. The sooner we get him the information, the sooner Nina will be exonerated." And Michelle would probably get a police guard.

"And, Frank," I said, "you and Bernard are going to have to tell Nina the truth."

Frank lowered his head in thought, staring at his shoe. "I don't know..." His voice trailed off.

"If Michelle knows, then chances are good Nina will find out. Think how she'd feel if she found out from someone else."

He gave a long, discernable sigh. "You're right. You set up the time and place, Tommi."

"I don't need to be included."

"Yes, I think you do. You're the peacemaker. If Nina should react badly, Bernard and I would probably act like a couple of dunces. She's become very fond of you, and I think you can help smooth things over. Please do that for me."

"All right, Frank. If you think I can help." Since I had unearthed all the truth that was so damaging, I'd do whatever I could to begin the healing.

I had not been in the office of Carruthers, Mierjeski and Poag since before the divorce. I never would have recognized it. Formerly decorated in a heavily masculine style, it was now much lighter and brighter, in deference, I supposed, to the number of women joining the firm. The color scheme was mauve and moss green and the furnishings were modern, though not stridently so.

"I'm here to see Bernard Poag," I told the receptionist whom I'd never seen before.

"Do you have an appointment?" She had no idea who I was.

"No. But it's quite urgent."

"Your name?"

"Mrs. Tommi Poag."

The receptionist did a double take, momentarily flustered, then regained her composure. She called Bernard over the intercom and forwarded my urgent message.

"Go right on down. Second door on the left." She gestured toward the hall to her left.

By the time I arrived at Bernard's office, he was standing in the doorway. "Come in. Have a seat." He gestured toward the wingback chair in front of his desk, still covered in the same striped fabric though more faded and worn than when I had last seen it. He had somehow resisted the office redo. But then he'd always clung to the old, worn pieces even at home.

"What's up?" he asked, shuffling papers on his desk to signal he didn't have time for chitchat.

"Michelle killed Cap and Daniel. And she tried twice to kill me." I said it matter-of-factly.

That got his attention. He looked up at me, his face registering total surprise. "Michelle? That's totally unbelievable!"

"She's in the hospital now. She tried to kill herself." And I relayed the whole tale of Michelle's affair with Cap and how it led to his death, as well as Daniel's murder and the two attempts on my own life. I handed him the headlight protector, and told him where I had found it.

"I'm speechless." Bernard sat back in his swivel chair and stared at a pen that he held poised between thumb and finger of each hand, running his fingers back and forth on its surface. "My sources had come up with some information on the witness that could impeach his credibility, but frankly we hadn't considered her own sister. That was some piece of investigation, Tommi. I guess I should have given you more consideration. But, you understand. Without credentials..."

This would have been such a sweet moment if only things hadn't turned out the way they did. I was elated that I could help Nina, but the fact that Michelle was guilty diminished my gratification considerably. Particularly because Frank was so devastated by it.

"There's one more thing that needs to be addressed," I said.

"What's that?"

"Michelle found out the truth about you and Marilyn. Her mother told her just before she died."

Bernard very slowly sat up straight and laid the pen down on his blotter. He looked at me without speaking, though he couldn't suppress the look of guilt that crossed his features.

"You're going to have to tell Nina," I continued. "She's bound to find out, and it would be so much better coming from you."

Bernard turned his chair around and stared out the window for a few minutes. Finally he turned back toward me. "What about Frank?"

"I think you should tell her together. You both love her. If you can convince her of that, maybe it won't hurt so much."

Bernard signed resignedly. "I guess I knew it was inevitable. Tell Frank I'd like to get it over with as soon as possible. I'll pass all this information on to the D.A. immediately."

"Frank wants me to be there too, if that's all right with you. Why don't you get things straightened out with the D.A. then give us a call at the hospital. We could meet you at Nina's house." I thought he would object to my presence, but he surprised me.

"Sounds like a good plan. I'll call you as soon as I can," Bernard said rising from his chair to show me out. He'd regained his cool exterior, giving no clue whether he felt embarrassment, remorse, or any other human emotion.

Back at the hospital, Frank and I went to the cafeteria for supper. Over meatloaf I reviewed my meeting with Bernard.

"What was his reaction when you said we needed to tell Nina?" Frank asked.

"He was acquiescent. No hedging. For one moment I thought I saw a flicker of remorse on his face. It didn't last long, But for Bernard, it was surprising."

"You mean old Stoneface?"

"You got it."

Then we returned to Michelle's room, sitting quietly as she slept. A nurse came in, smiling broadly at me, and I suddenly realized it was Evelyn Truesdale.

"I heard you were here," Evelyn said. "I came to tell you the autopsy report came back on Oscar Sellars."

"Evelyn," I said, "this is Frank Poag, Nina's father." I felt a shiver now that I would always wonder if he really was.

"Oh, Mr. Poag," Evelyn said shaking his hand. "So sorry about Nina. Do you remember me? I used to babysit her."

Frank concentrated on her face for several seconds trying to recall her. "Yes, that's right. You lived around the corner from us on Archdale."

"I moved about the time Nina was nine or ten. That's why I don't know Michelle." She nodded her head toward the bed.

"Tell us about the autopsy," I said, losing patience. Enough of this chitchat. After all, Evelyn was the one who hinted that Nina might have killed Cap in the hospital.

"Oh, yes. It seems Cap had a heart attack. The autopsy showed he had heart disease and the near-drowning must have triggered the attack. It was massive and instantaneous. And I was sorry to hear about Michelle," Evelyn added, glancing again toward the sleeping figure. "She must have been very upset over Nina." It was obvious she was fishing for the whole story.

But neither Frank nor I had any intention of enlightening her. She'd find out soon enough. We just nodded and murmured, "Yes, poor Michelle."

Evelyn fussed about Michelle's bed, prolonging her visit till she realized we would say no more.

Shortly after she left, Bernard called to say he could meet us at Nina's about nine. He said he'd already called her and told her to expect him, not mentioning that the two of us would be there too.

Bernard's car was in the driveway when we arrived. We let ourselves in and went to the family room where Bernard and Nina were talking together.

"Dad! Tommi! Where have you guys been all day?" Nina asked. "That lady you hired to do housework was not very efficient, and it was like I couldn't get rid of her. She kept claiming she had more to do, more to do. In fact she didn't leave till Bernard came. What kind of agency did you hire her through anyway?"

Frank sat beside her with a guilty smile. "That was no housekeeper. That was a former lady marine that I hired to keep an eye on you."

Nina laughed. "Oh, I see. Now it all becomes clear. She'd never make a living cleaning houses, let me tell you."

Bernard stood up, assuming his best courtroom stance. "I haven't told her yet. Wanted to wait for you."

"Told me what?" Nina looked alarmed.

"Good news, honey," Frank said. "The case has been solved. You are off the hook." He turned to look at me. "Your friend here gets all the credit." Together the men went step by step through the events of the past week, putting all the puzzle pieces in place. When Nina learned who was responsible, she was devastated. She cried copious tears, both in relief for her own exoneration, and in grief for the sister who betrayed her.

Finally she calmed down and went to wash her face in the bathroom. "Okay, Frank," Bernard said while she was gone, "let's get this other thing over with. I think you should tell the story, and don't mince any words about me. I deserve whatever I get."

Bernard must have had some kind of a religious conversion. I couldn't believe my ears!

When Nina returned, Frank began. "There's something else you must know. And I guess I've been elected to tell you. Just before your mom and I were married, we had a huge fight." He paused to gather courage and Nina looked at him curiously. "She found comfort in Bernard at that time." His voice was so soft, I wondered if Nina heard him or understood what he was saying. He hurried on. "But we made up and went ahead with the wedding. You were born less than nine months later."

Nina stared at him, frowning in attempt to comprehend his meaning. She looked at Bernard for enlightenment, but he said nothing.

"In other words," Frank said in a wavering voice, "we're not sure which of us is your father."

Nina said nothing for a minute as the impact of his revelation became clear. Finally she said in a small voice, "Why are you telling me this?"

"Because Michelle knows," Bernard said. "Your mother told her just before she died. If your sister knows, then you should too."

Nina looked from Frank to Bernard to Frank again in disbelief. I was poised to comfort her, but she seemed too stunned for tears. Just when it seemed that she was unwilling to accept the news and might even bolt from the room, she began to speak. "What can I say? You just blew me away with this. But, the fact is I love you both. And I want you to end your feud. I've hated that you've refused to speak all these years. But now that I know the truth, I can't bear the thought of you hating each other. I want you to make up."

The men looked at each other, then at Nina.

"You're right. It's gone on far too long," Frank said.

Bernard nodded in agreement. "We've acted like children. It's time we grew up."

Nina got up and gave each of them a hug and a kiss. "We could probably solve all this through DNA. But you know what? I think it'd be better to leave well enough alone. I'll think of both of you as my dads. You both have been so good to me."

"You look tired," Frank told her. "I think we should go now."

"Thanks, Dad...Frank," she said and smiled.

The three of us left and Frank drove me back to my motel. "This has been some day," he said as he pulled up in front of Mi Casa. "I know my life will never be the same. I'm so worried about Michelle. I hope she gets the help she needs."

"We'll do everything we can to help her," I answered. "I feel this is a turning point in my life too. I have such mixed emotions about how it all turned out. I'm proud and happy I could help Nina, but hated that you've been hurt by it."

He put his arm around my shoulder. "I've been through hard times before. I guess I can survive this."

We sat quietly for several minutes, my head on Frank's shoulder. Finally I spoke. "There's one unequivocally good thing that came out of all this."

"What's that?"

"It gave us the opportunity to meet."

He put his hand under my chin, tilted my head up and kissed me tenderly. "I'll have to say I agree with you one hundred percent on that."